Tiger's Eye

Also by Barbra Annino

Opal Fire: Stacy Justice Book One

Bloodstone: Stacy Justice Book Two

Gnome Wars: A Short Story

Every Witch Way But Wicked: An Anthology
(includes a Stacy Justice story)

My Guardian Idiot—fantasy tales to tickle your funny bone

BOOK THREE OF THE STACY JUSTICE SERIES

Tiger's Eye

(It is highly recommended
that this series be read in order.)

Barbra Annino

The characters and events portrayed in this book are fictitious. Any similarity to real persons, living or dead, is coincidental and not intended by the author.

Published by Thomas & Mercer
P.O. Box 400818
Las Vegas, NV 89140

ISBN-13: 9781612186146
ISBN-10: 1612186149

Dedication

Dedicated to four-legged friends everywhere
and those who love them.
And, as always, for George.

Prologue

(from the last scene of *BLOODSTONE*)

Chance walked into my office and said, "Hey, gorgeous. You ready?" He came over and brushed his lips across my neck. Then he sat on my desk and pulled me to him.

I stood, draped my arms around his neck, and kissed him thoroughly.

"What do you say we get some takeout and go to my place?"

"Only if it involves chocolate syrup," I said.

"Oh, that could be arranged."

I leaned across my desk to grab my bag and the phone rang.

"Don't answer it," Chance said.

I smiled. "Two minutes."

The voice on the other end of the line was gruff. "Stacy Justice?"

"Speaking."

"Stacy Justice the second, right?"

"Yes."

Chance tickled me and I laughed.

"I just thought you should know that I have the tapes."

"What tapes?" I asked, slapping Chance's hands away.

The man on the phone swore softly. "You haven't gone through his files yet, have you?"

"Whose files? What you are talking about?"

Chance looked at me, concerned. He raised his hand, questioningly. I shrugged.

"It wasn't an accident," the man said.

I sat down in my chair, that creepy-crawly feeling climbing up my spine. "Who is this?"

"Your father was murdered."

Then he hung up.

Chapter I

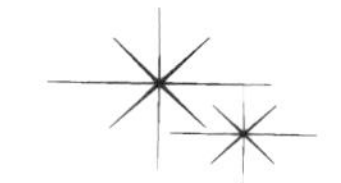

"It's a dog-eat-dog world and I'm wearing Milkbone underwear."

—Norm Peterson, *Cheers*

If my high school softball coach could see me now, she would probably take a bat to my kneecaps. Not because I was wearing the most hideous pink uniform outside of *Toddlers and Tiaras,* or because I had struck out twice already, but because the opposing team consisted mostly of geriatrics slathered in mentholated ointment. And they were kicking my ass.

"Next up in the batter's box, head reporter of the *Amethyst Globe,* one-time record holder of most pop-ups in a single game, the master of disaster, the ultimate witchcrafter—"

"Gus," I hissed, "enough!"

The guy on the bullhorn was Gus Dorsey, a man with all the charm and wit of Mr. Potato Head. He stood a foot away, dressed in striped knee-high socks and shorts last seen on *Magnum P.I.* Either they were hand-me-downs from his father or Gus was dabbling in the retro look.

"Stacy Justice, folks." He lowered the horn and looked at me as if I had just spit on his ice cream.

Now I felt bad. Gus had droopy eyes and floppy ears so even in his happiest moments he gave the appearance of a Muppet that didn't make the cut.

I put my beer down and grabbed the horn. "Thank you, Officer Dorsey. How about a hand for those who protect and serve?" I said to the crowd.

Claps and cheers drifted from the bleachers and I turned to wave until I noticed there was a turtle race going on with money exchanging hands. A quick glance at Gus told me that he would allow such infractions to slide on this, the Founder's Day of Amethyst, Illinois.

The baseball bats were stacked outside the dugout and I grabbed one that I hadn't used yet in hopes of improving my average. I took a few swings to get the weight and rhythm of the wood, stepping onto the freshly cut grass. The sun felt like a warm massage on my exposed arms and the air was bursting with the aroma of grilled hamburgers and buttery popcorn. Off in the distance, I heard the squeals of delighted children winning prizes.

In the Midwest, you cling to the days of cookouts, block parties, and county fairs. When light lingers in the sky and the earth is fertile for weeks to come—promising a bounty of vine-ripened tomatoes and bunches of fresh herbs—there is a sense that anything could happen.

Anything at all.

I stepped toward home plate, tipping my head to Shea Parker, my boss, who was standing off the first base line.

He flashed me some hand signals.

I had no idea what he was doing. I flicked my eyes to Derek, my coworker and the paper's photographer. He rolled his eyes in return and leaned back against the brick wall of the dugout. He pulled his cap over his smooth, dark face and folded his arms.

Parker rushed over to me and signaled to Gus, who was not only the announcer and scorekeeper but also the umpire.

"You calling a time-out?" Gus asked.

"Just give me a minute," Parker said.

"What?" My beer was getting warm and this game was getting old. Normally, I was all for sports. My body felt better when it was fit, and I enjoyed the friendly camaraderie of a pick-up game. But I had a lot on my mind today thanks to a creepy phone call I'd received at the office the day before. So I just wanted to grab a burger, suck down some beers, relax at a picnic bench, and enjoy the beautiful sunshine. For once, I wanted to do what I wanted and not what everyone else expected of me.

Maybe that was selfish, but we all need *me* time now and then.

"You are not taking this seriously. Don't you remember the signals?"

"Sorry, I don't."

"That's because you only came to two practices." Parker held up two fingers as a visual aid.

Only two? I spent five days a week with the man. Since he was my editor, that was a job requirement. Wearing this stupid neon jersey with a matching headband was not. The uniform wasn't his fault, though. I had Gladys, the research assistant for the *Amethyst Globe*, to thank for that. She'd been tasked with outfitting the team and her favorite color was fuchsia.

I sighed. "Just tell me. What do you want me to do?"

He craned his neck around, nervously eyeing the field behind him.

"What is the big deal? It's a charity game, for crying out loud," I said.

Parker shuffled a bit. He leaned in and said softly, "With you and Derek, I might finally win one of these things."

"Fine. What's the plan?"

"Bunt."

I nodded, and looked at my opponents.

The game was an annual Founder's Day event. The sponsorships and donations supported extracurricular activities for the local schools. Kids counted on that money every year. With the state slashing budgets for sports and the arts, communities like ours were forced to fund those projects via taxpayers and events such as these.

But it wasn't like you got a bonus for winning.

Most of the players were local business owners and their employees. The teams were usually chosen at random, but this year someone decided that it would be a great idea if tavern, restaurant, and B&B owners went up against bankers, realtors, and newspaper staff.

In other words, nine-to-fivers vs. hospitality folks.

Which pretty much pitted me against my whole family.

I kicked my cleats against the dirt and surveyed the field. Cinnamon, my cousin and the owner of the Black Opal Bar and Grill, crouched at first base like a bear protecting her cub. A local restaurant owner guarded second, and Monique, proprietor of Down and Dirty nightclub, was way out in left field adjusting her right boob.

I stepped into the batter's box and arched the bat behind me. Lolly, my great-aunt, grinned up at me from her position as catcher. Her face was slashed with black ink that football players used to keep the sun from their eyes. She wore a white tennis skirt, saddle shoes, and a sequined tube top with a red bra fastened over it.

My grandmother, Birdie, was on the mound. I had never seen her in Spandex. Hopefully I never would again.

Birdie lowered her head and hinged forward, eyes glued to her eldest sister. The sun penetrated her coppery waves, lending her hair an iridescent shine. She paused, nodded at Lolly, then wound up, took a step back, and fired the ball through the air.

It was about to enter that sweet spot just above my waist, just where I liked it. Then, as I was poised to crack it over her head (bunting was never going to happen), the ball dove up—as if mocking me—and charged straight into Lolly's mitt.

"Strike one!" yelled Gus.

Dizzy from the force of a failed hit, I wondered, *What the hell happened?* The ball had been right over the plate.

I stretched my arms briefly, shook my shoulders and hands, before stepping back inside the box.

A glimmer in Birdie's emerald eyes gave me pause. Had she done something to that ball? Would she cheat?

I shot back a fierce glare, hoping my own eyes—a lighter green than hers—appeared as cold as a shark's. My head nodded slightly.

I know what you're up to, old lady, and it won't work. You've been training me, yes, but I'm younger, stronger, and faster. I don't need magic to win.

Laughter. Loud, clear, and very familiar. Only it wasn't external. She was literally inside my head. I smacked my ear to shake her out.

So, she was going to play dirty. Well, two could play at that game.

I steeled myself, flexed my biceps, and curled my lip up in a snarl.

This time, Birdie did a full 360-degree spin and launched the ball. It was coming over the plate, right into range. I swung. Hard.

The damn thing twirled around the bat, hit the wood, then bounced off the far fence and rolled into Lolly's glove.

I stepped out of the box. "Cut that out, Lolly!" I pointed to Birdie. "You too!"

She had to be using magic. There was no physical explanation for how that ball moved.

Lolly gave me a sinister smile.

Parker was cheering me on. "Come on, Stacy. Bring it home. You've got two strikes and no balls."

He was right about one thing. I had two strikes. "Time!"

Gus came over and dusted off home plate.

Lolly stood and cracked her neck. She pulled out a silver flask with her initials engraved on it and downed a shot. Jameson, from the smell of it. I could only imagine how many she had belted for breakfast to play so sharply.

Normally, she functioned like a hot air balloon with a faulty pilot light, but alcohol acted as brain fuel for Aunt Lolly.

Parker came over and asked what the problem was.

"She's cheating!" I pointed at Lolly. "Gus, tell her to knock it off. She put some sort of sp…" I was going to say spell, but I chewed the word off and came up with "*spin* on it."

It wasn't exactly a secret—my family of witches. Most people in town knew what we were, even accepted it. But I was still warming up to the idea. Still wrapping my brain around all that had transpired in the year since I had been back home.

As a reporter, I relied on facts, not the fantastical.

As a woman raised by witches who considered me the Seeker of Justice, I had to face the very real, unexplainable events that happened around me far too often.

It wasn't easy, but I was getting there with the guidance of my grandmother and her two sisters. Not to mention the Blessed Book of our theology and family history. It contained not only spellcraft, herbal remedies, and recipes, but predictions for future generations (hence the Seeker of Justice title I now carried) and the history of my ascendants, whose roots reached back to an ancient tribe of Druids from County Kildare, Ireland. The book had been passed from Maegan, Birdie's mother (who also helped me out on occasion, though she was long dead) to Birdie. Now it belonged to me.

"Now, Stacy," Gus said, "don't be a sore loser."

Aunt Lolly stuck her tongue out at me.

See, when they acted like escaped mental patients, my faith wavered.

Gus stepped in before I kicked dirt all over the catcher. "Your aunt Lolly was MVP of the farm league four years running. Of course she might play better than you."

My mouth dropped. "She was? I never knew that."

Parker and Gus both looked at me as if I were the worst grandchild on earth.

"Your grandma Birdie too. She was home-run queen." Parker scratched his chin. "Fiona played some ball as well, but she mostly looked gorgeous in the uniform. Don't tell me you've never even seen the photos?"

Aunt Fiona did a beauty pageant wave from third base, wiggling her hips and showing off her supple legs. It was my belief that most garages in this town had been plastered with her pinup at one time or another.

I shook my head. "Fine." I stepped back up to the plate and Lolly repositioned herself.

This time when the ball came at me, I took two hop steps toward it—before it got near Lolly—and smacked a line drive over Birdie's head.

I tossed the bat and ran as fast as I could. Cinnamon leaned in to field the catch. I was a few inches taller than my cousin, but she was a powerhouse of a woman. If Cinnamon were a car, she'd be a Challenger with flames painted on the side and a Hemi under the hood.

First base was three steps away. I could smell the sweetness of victory as I pumped my legs. Cin reached to catch the ball and her foot slipped off the bag.

There was no choice.

I had to slide.

Which was a much easier task for a teenager than a woman in the twilight of her twenties.

My arms stretched out in front of me as my chest skidded across the dirt. My chin bounced off a rock before my body came to a complete stop.

There is no way to describe the taste of dirt. It just tastes brown. But the salty taste of my own sweat mixed with the metallic flavor of the blood leaking from the bite in my lip definitely added to the buffet going on in my mouth.

I felt leather and I yelped in excitement. At least I had reached the base.

"Out!" yelled Gus.

What the…? "Are you freaking kidding me? Doesn't the tie go to the runner?" I said, barely lifting my head.

"Um, Cuz?" Cinnamon said.

I looked up. My hand was touching her shoe. "Son of a bitch."

Cinnamon helped me to my feet, a brief look of horror crossing her face.

"What?"

"I don't think they make Band-Aids that big, Stace."

I looked down. I was a walking road rash.

Gus got on his horn again. "Well, that's it for the eighth inning, folks. Let's give our teams a hand."

"You okay?" Cinnamon asked me.

"I'll be fine."

She patted my back and jogged toward the dugout as the crowd clapped without enthusiasm.

Parker walked over with a cold beer and a wet towel. I thanked him, drank half the beer, washed up, and tossed the towel. There was hardly any skin left on my knees and they stung like hell.

Derek was our team's first baseman and he was kind enough to bring me my mitt as he took position.

"Really?" was all he said.

"They were cheating. It was my best option."

"And you care why?"

Good question, but not good enough to warrant a response. I put my glove on and carried the rest of my beer toward right field.

My bear of a Great Dane trotted over and sat in front of me, defiantly blocking my path.

"Hi, Thor."

He gave me a pitiful look as if to say he was incredibly disappointed. Thor could be rather competitive when it came to sports. You don't want to see him on a volleyball court.

"I'm sorry, buddy. I didn't even get us on base. My bad."

He grumbled, his black muzzle moving in waves over his sharp canines. He licked my right knee and stood, his giant head anchored regally above his massive tan frame.

"Tell you what, big guy, you get us three up, three down and I will not only buy you the biggest hot dog they have in that tent, I'll take you swimming tomorrow. Okay?"

He considered this, then howled in approval.

"Great. High five."

I lifted my right arm and Thor reared up to meet it with his left paw, towering a full foot over me. His landing shook the ground and he trotted over to his place at short-stop.

Making my way to center field, I finished the icy cold brew and tossed the cup toward the back woods, where I would retrieve it after the inning. The lake was just beyond the forest and I could hear splashing and screaming.

But not the screams of playful children.

It was a man's scream.

A terrified scream.

I spun around to face the infield, but it seemed that no one else heard the cries, not even Thor, whose ears were perked and pointed toward the plate, where Cinnamon was gearing up to bat.

Had I imagined it?

I looked back toward the giant oak tree that stood at the edge of the park. There, lounging on a thick bough, was a sleek white tiger with ebony stripes. She had piercing eyes the color of the Caribbean Sea and she aimed her gaze right at me. Her whiskers flickered and her tail slapped the branch once, punctuating her presence.

Before I could process what I was seeing and the meaning behind it, Parker yelled, "Stacy!"

I whirled to see Thor charging my way and a high fly targeting my head. I dodged left just in time to miss the full impact of my two-hundred-pound dog as he leaped into the air to make the catch. He tagged me only with his back legs, which was enough to knock me down, but not enough to knock the wind out of me, thankfully.

Thor sauntered over to me, ball in his mouth, and lowered his neck. I grabbed his collar and pulled myself up. He looked at me proudly and I praised him.

Then Cinnamon screamed, "Dammit, Thor, no more rides in the new convertible for you!"

Thor whined and moped back to the pitcher's mound, depositing the ball at Parker's feet. My boss patted the dog's head, picked up the ball, and wiped it off with his shirt.

When I looked back, the tiger was gone.

Chapter 2

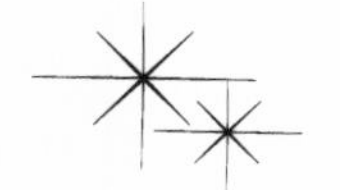

"A hot dog at the game beats roast beef at the Ritz."
—Humphrey Bogart

Despite the short-stop's valiant effort, we lost 10–2. As promised, Thor and I made our way over to the grill and I bought us each a hot dog. One with sauerkraut, one with mustard. I'll let you figure out whose was whose.

I grabbed a water and a beer (for myself) at the neighboring tent, hydrated the dog, and made my way over to a weathered picnic table already claimed by Birdie and the aunts. En route, I spotted Cinnamon accosting a clown near the cotton candy station so I walked over to see if I could help. The clown, not my cousin.

Her voice was raised, her face twisted in anger. "Listen, Bozo, I said I don't want a freaking balloon. I don't care what animal you can turn it into. Now get out of my way before I tie your nuts in a knot."

The poor guy was about Cin's height, which was to say he was slightly taller than a member of the Lollipop Guild. He looked to me for help.

"How much?" I asked.

"It's only five dollars. It's for the kids." He had a nasal voice and watery eyes. Not to mention a big red nose.

"I'll give you ten dollars to stay twenty feet away from this woman at all times."

We made the deal and Cinnamon gave the guy an Italian hand gesture.

It wasn't her fault, really. Cinnamon has had a great fear of clowns ever since she was robbed by one in New Orleans on her honeymoon.

The way her husband, Tony, explained it to me, the newlyweds were standing outside of Café Du Monde, about ready to take a romantic carriage ride across the city when a seemingly innocuous clown approached them. He was a smooth-talker, telling my cousin what a beautiful woman she was while distracting her with fast-moving hands and shiny balloons. At the end of his spiel, Cinnamon was up one blue giraffe and down one engagement ring.

Being recently married and being Cinnamon, she noticed the absence of the ring immediately. A police report corroborated what happened next.

In her defense, Cin gave the clown one chance to rectify the situation. When he denied all knowledge of the missing ring, Cin literally took the law into her own hands by grabbing the guy's collar with one hand—nearly lifting him off the ground—and shaking him down with the other. She tore through his apron, tossing tiny scraps of colored latex all over Decatur Street, destroying the seeds of dozens of potential balloon animals. When she finally heard the ring drop, she released the clown and bent down to pick it up. She held it to his face, waiting for an apology or, at the very least, admission of guilt.

The poor bastard still denied taking it.

His nose is permanently red and Cinnamon isn't allowed near the Big Easy.

"You okay?" I asked her.

Cin was shaking. "I hate clowns."

I hugged her. "Who doesn't?"

I handed Thor his hot dog and he lumbered over to a shady spot and sat down to eat. My cousin and I approached our grandmother and the aunts and scooted onto the bench.

"Anastasia," Birdie said.

"Grandmother," I said.

Birdie stiffened and I couldn't help but grin. She was proud of the fact that she was named after the goddess Brighid, keeper of the hearth and fire. She hated being called grandmother as much as I hated being called Anastasia. Especially since my birth name was Stacy.

"Aren't you going to congratulate us?" Fiona asked in that sultry voice that made her sound like she should be draped over a piano.

"You cheated." I bit into my hot dog.

Fiona looked shocked. She put a hand to her ample bosom. "Well, that is a terrible thing to say, young lady."

Always with the theatrics, these three.

I swigged some beer. "Okay, maybe not you." I pointed from Birdie to Lolly. "But you two. I'm almost positive."

"Oh, you think you have it all figured out, do you?" Birdie was sitting across from me and she leaned forward.

"Perhaps there are things about your family that you don't know, Miss Smart Aleck."

That was the understatement of the year. For instance, until a few months ago I thought my mother had run off and left me at the age of fourteen. Turned out, she was incarcerated in Ireland by some sort of pagan council that abided Celtic law—a wrong I intended to right on the next Samhain when her parole would be considered. And let's not forget all these years I was under the misconception that my father's death had been an accident. But with that phone call yesterday—and the vision of the tiger today—now I wasn't so sure.

Of course, that wasn't what Birdie meant.

"So what's all this about you three playing on some farm league? And why did I not know about it? I mean, you taught me all about the Celtic triads, the best time of the year for moon magic, how to cleanse a circle with rosemary, and all the other rules of the craft, but no one thought I might be interested in learning how to throw a curve ball?"

The three of them looked at each other like confused kittens with too many balls of yarn to unravel.

Lolly adjusted her cap. "It never occurred to us, dear. You were born for bigger things." She somehow managed to remove the tube top, leaving only her bra to cover her upper half.

Cinnamon stifled a laugh next to me. I never understood why they didn't recruit her into their familial coven, but if the Blessed Book was the baseline for all things witchy, it might be due to the fact that her father was my mother's brother. Geraghty "gifts" were passed maternally, so perhaps Birdie decided that magic wasn't in my cousin's blood.

Not that it provided much comfort. Sometimes I really wished I had a cohort in all this. Especially those days when it felt like it was me against the Geraghty Girls. Which was pretty much every day.

"Speaking of bigger things," Birdie said, "what happened in the outfield? You seemed...distracted."

They all looked at me. I hadn't told anyone yet about the mysterious phone call I had received. Not even Chance, my high school sweetheart and current flame, who happened to be there at the time. The caller told me my father was murdered and he mentioned something about tapes. I shrugged it off, thinking it was most likely some nutjob making a prank call.

But then I saw the tiger. And that itchy, twitchy sensation was creeping up on me—the one that warned of trouble on the horizon.

However, it was Saturday, the sun was shining, the beer was cold, and we were celebrating an event that came around only once a year. And with the summer solstice approaching, I knew they would recruit me for projects to prepare for the ritual night.

Today I just wanted a stress-free zone, so I shrugged and told Birdie I was watching a frolicking pair of squirrels.

She didn't believe me and maybe she didn't press it for the same reasons I didn't want to discuss it. Or maybe she was high off her victory.

In hindsight, had I told her the truth right then and there, fewer people might have died.

Chapter 3

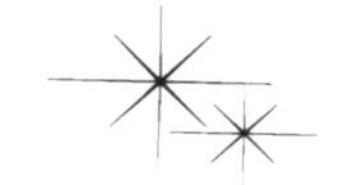

"I spilled spot remover on my dog. He's gone now."
—Steven Wright

After consuming our weight in junk food and playing Ring Toss, Shoot the Clown (Cin's idea), and Balloon Darts, Cinnamon left to go find Tony and I climbed on top of the same picnic table I had shared with Birdie earlier. She, along with Lolly and Fiona, had called it a day hours ago. The old oak was in my line of sight, its gnarled branches reaching out to caress the sky. I stared at it, attempting to conjure up the ethereal tiger, but saw nothing.

What was she trying to tell me?

She had visited me once—months ago—via a mirror in Birdie's house. It was right before I was about to embark on a task given to me by my grandmother. One I couldn't exactly refuse under the circumstances. A girl's life was at stake.

One I would never forget either because before then, I was what you might consider a nonbeliever.

Now, I guess, I was a bendable skeptic.

There are things in this world even the brightest minds cannot explain. There is no denying that. I've heard it said that magic is science that hasn't been discovered yet. Somehow, that sentiment was comforting to me.

What made me *uncomfortable* was my role in this supernatural realm. Or my grandmother's perception of my role. Birdie thought (because of something her mother, Maegan, had written in the Blessed Book) that I was the Seeker of Justice for my generation.

Never mind that there was no explanation for what that meant. Never mind that the passage she extracted this nugget of knowledge from was as generic as a greeting card. Or that perhaps it was a coincidence my father's surname was Justice.

Never mind all that. What scared the living hell out of me was that if there was even the slightest chance that this were true—that my calling was to fulfill Old World prophesies and protect sacred truths—then frankly, I sucked at it.

Sure, I had uncovered some heinous crimes done by horrible people, but what did that matter if I couldn't save the ones I loved? If this whole Seeker thing really belonged to me, then dammit, I wanted to help those I cared about, not random strangers I never met.

Maybe that sounded selfish too. But there it was.

Oscar Wilde wrote, "To lose one parent may be regarded as a misfortune; to lose both looks like carelessness." That pretty much summed it up for me.

How could I have lost them both? My mother to the council for a crime she committed to protect me and my father to…to…what? Murder?

How could I have not seen that coming? If it were true. And if it weren't, I had still misread the dream about the accident that killed him.

Either way, I screwed up.

As I gazed at the sky, feeling bitter and angry with myself, a gust of wind washed through the park, knocking my beer over. It sloshed across the bench and dripped down my leg in a single, narrow stream. I used my headband to wipe it away, tossed it aside, and gazed upward.

I sighed at the moon. "Am I overthinking this?"

"Probably," Chance said behind me and I yelped.

"Sorry. Didn't mean to scare you." He slid his arms around my waist and touched his cheek to mine, gently rocking me to the tune of Guns and Roses' "Sweet Child o' Mine," drifting over from the band tent.

Chance kissed my neck in a way that made my entire body shudder.

"What are you overthinking, Stacy?" he asked.

I enveloped his arms in mine and said, "Nothing important."

He kissed my neck again, lower this time, and a shiver bolted through my chest.

"That's a bright star." He pointed over my right shoulder.

"That's not a star, that's Venus."

"Planet of love, right?"

"Hmm-hmm." Suddenly I was so tired I could hardly stand. I leaned into him, let the strength of him carry me, if only for a moment.

"You want to dance?" he asked.

"I think I just want to go home, take a hot shower, and crawl into bed."

He tilted my face to him and said, “That can be arranged, my lady.”

I stood and Chance lifted me off the bench. He was wearing a blue sleeveless shirt that matched his eyes and his biceps swelled as he held me in the air. My legs found their way around his waist as I entwined my fingers in his sandy hair. I smiled down at him as he held me up by my thighs.

“You have sauerkraut in your teeth,” he teased.

“I probably smell like beer too.” I dropped my head.

“Wanna know something?” he asked.

I peeked at him through my bangs.

“I love sauerkraut and beer.” He kissed me gently and I slid down his body, slowly, enjoying the friction between our bare legs until my feet found the earth.

“Where’s the big man?” Chance asked, grabbing my backpack. He knocked my cleats against the bench to loosen the dirt and shoved them inside. I was glad I had brought a change of clothes because that polyester uniform would have been hell to walk around in all day.

I looked around. “Now that you mention it, I haven’t seen him in a while. Derek took him over near the puppet show to play with the kids.”

Thor loved to ham it up for the neighborhood munchkins. His parlor tricks kept them entertained, and in return he received an endless supply of belly rubs and whatever food fell from their hands. It was a win-win. I called his name and waited for him to lope over to me, expecting him to be spent from an afternoon of overindulgence and exercise.

He didn’t respond to my calls.

I looked at Chance. “That’s odd.”

"He's probably snoring away on some poor schmuck's lap. I'll check the far end near the band and the beer tent and you take the concession stands," Chance said.

We separated, each calling my dog's name.

I hadn't realized how many food vendors there were earlier when my cousin and I were eating our way through the festival. Hot dogs, bratwurst, burgers, funnel cakes, popcorn, ice cream, cotton candy, and deep-fried Snickers bars were just a few of the menu items.

I felt a little nauseous then. I normally don't eat like a defensive line backer with hypoglycemia, but something about summertime did that to me.

I kept my eyes peeled for a pony-sized dog everywhere I turned, hoping to spot him snoozing under a tent or sticking out of a garbage can, searching for a half-eaten pork sandwich.

Neither scenario came to fruition.

Leo, the chief of police and my former beau, emerged from behind the snow cone machine just then. He was wearing a white T-shirt and khaki shorts that were glued to him because he was sopping wet. The way his nearly black hair was slicked back, he looked like he should be sporting a tommy gun and a zoot suit.

"What happened to you?" I asked.

"Dunk tank. By the way, your grandmother has a killer fast ball." He wrung his shirt out, exposing a hint of chiseled abs and a small tuft of hair that trailed down his navel. "And a mean streak. She must have dunked me twelve times before she ran out of cash."

I think Birdie would have preferred it if I were asexual like a tulip. Or a tapeworm. All this nonsense with dating got in the way of her grand plan for me to become some sort of superhero, battling Evil and Idiots so she could have the privilege of adding the juiciest chapter of all to the Blessed Book of the Geraghty clan. Because, you know, my accomplishments were also hers.

"Sorry about that."

He shrugged. "It's for a good cause." He looked past me, his dark lashes clumped like stars around his eyes. "Where's Chance?" he asked, smiling one of those awkward, gritting-your-teeth smiles that you do when you run into your ex and feel forced to make polite conversation.

I couldn't blame him for being hurt or angry. Things hadn't ended badly between us, they just ended, partly due to circumstances, partly thanks to the cruelty of fate. Leo was a great guy—sexy as hell, funny, and kind. But dating a police officer has serious disadvantages when you come from a family of witches and you may or may not have a secret identity that requires you to guard ancient artifacts, protect unclaimed treasures, and occasionally break the law while dressed like Catwoman.

A girlfriend like that could really ruin the career of a guy in law enforcement. So I had to let him go.

"Actually he's looking for Thor. Have you seen him?"

Leo thought for a moment. "Last time I saw him, some kid was torturing him by making him balance a hot dog on his nose."

"How long did he hold out?"

"About forty-five seconds."

"I think that's a record."

Leo laughed. "I'll help you look. Let me just change. I'll catch up with you." He pointed a duffel bag toward the restrooms.

I thanked him and felt a little sad as he trotted off. I hated to think that I had hurt him. I said a silent prayer to Venus to find someone for him. Someone suited to him the way Chance and I were suited.

I turned the corner and spotted Derek talking to a woman just outside of the tent where the band was jamming away. I waved to him and he waved me away, turning sideways so he could properly hit on the cute blonde.

I tapped him on the shoulder. "Excuse me." He pretended not to hear, see, or feel me.

I said to her freckled face, "May I borrow him for two seconds?"

"Sure," she said.

Derek spun around and glared at me. I pinched his shoulder and pulled him forward.

"You trippin', woman. Why you always crunching my mojo?"

"I don't even know what that means and stop talking like you're all gangsta." I flashed my hands for emphasis. "You're from Connecticut for crissakes. Your father is an investment banker, your mom spearheads about a hundred charity events, and your sister is in law school. Aside from your Voodoo priestess aunt down south, you're almost as white as I am."

Derek put his hand to the side of his mouth and I noticed his pants slipped farther down his legs as he made the gesture. He was also wearing his ball cap sideways.

“She’s into it. I think she’s got daddy issues. Likes the bad boys.” He cocked his brow.

Oh, for crying out loud. I flashed my eyes toward the girl who could have passed for Strawberry Shortcake. She was wearing a rockabilly dress in a cherry print with a gold cross around her neck. Her peep-toe platforms looked to be causing her great pain the way she kept shifting from one foot to the other. “How old is she?”

“Nineteen,” he said.

I wanted to tell him that a bottle of Boone’s Farm and a make-out session behind the church worked on any girl who was mad at Dad, but I decided that it was none of my business.

“Good luck with that, Jay-Z, but listen. I can’t find Thor. Have you seen him?”

“Not for about an hour.”

I chewed my lower lip, worrying myself into a frenzy. This wasn’t like Thor. Most days, the dog followed me around like I had rib eyes taped to my ass.

Where had he gotten off to?

“You want me to help you look for him?” Derek asked, not really meaning it.

“I appreciate the offer, but that’s okay. Chance and Leo are looking for him too. Have fun.”

I hurried away from the tent, growing a little more nauseous, not from the junk food, but from the fear of losing Thor. Birdie referred to him as my familiar, my protector, but he was also my family. What would I do if I lost Thor?

I started rushing around the park like a maniac, asking people if they had seen him. I lifted tent skirts, crawled under tables, leaned over gaming counters, and checked in the bushes.

All I found were a couple of teenagers making out, a pantless carny, and a passed-out clown clutching a forty-ounce Miller High Life.

When you're desperate, scared, and a little drunk, you do things you wouldn't normally do. Especially in the summer. Now, I should let you know that I had not danced naked under a Mead Moon since I was two. Even then, it was the night of the solstice and people expect it on that day. Well, my people anyway. I was also not a fan of practicing the craft outdoors in a wide-open field where any number of wanderers could not only interrupt the spell but contaminate it.

But like I said, I was desperate. And possibly a bit tipsy.

Chance still had my bag, which meant I had limited tools. There were no crystals, charms, or potions on me; however, I did have a silver key chain with the Black Opal's logo on it, a bottle of water, and that ever-present source for the most powerful spell casting there was—the moon.

Thor's collar was fastened with a tiger's eye, fully charged to accept magic. I knew he would receive the enchantment. All I had to do was perform it.

I rushed over to the towering oak and plucked a small bough to offer Diana, Greek goddess of the moon, huntress, and canine protector. I opened the bottle of water (the moon's favorite element), scanned the tree bed for the brightest beam, and balanced it there between two rocks. Next, I laid the key chain—widest chunk of silver aimed at the thickest slice of light—across the rocks, set the oak bough on top, and chanted three times:

"Diana, huntress of the night,
bring this canine back to sight.
Guided by the moonbeam's light,
friends be found without a fight."

I waited, listening to the sounds of the wind and the gentle sway of the leaves. I was hoping it would be instantaneous, but Thor didn't come bounding out of the woods.

Damn! I forgot to picture him in my mind as I cast the spell.

I centered myself again. Checked the position of the key chain, the water bottle, and the light of the moon.

Then, the largest oak leaf started smoldering. It cracked and hissed on top of the key chain. Finally, after a few more seconds of sputtering, it curled into itself, rose up in a puff of indigo smoke, and dissipated.

A sign. It worked!

I turned, a slow full circle, and called Thor's name.

Just off to my right, a patch of evergreens rustled.

"Thor?" I crept over to the shrubs and heard a squeaking sound. Out popped a Chihuahua smaller than Thor's nose. I swear the thing could have fit in my palm.

"Oh my goodness, you are the cutest!" I reached over to pick him up and the snarky little gnat nearly confiscated my index finger.

"Hey, that's not nice. Bad dog." I shook my finger at him to make a point.

Apparently the fact that I still had possession of the digit pissed him off. He lunged at my ankles with the ferocity of a bridezilla. I hopscotched around his teeth, trying not to squash him like a bug, but really wanting to.

Suddenly he stopped, stuck his nose in the air, and ran off to see what smelled so good.

I blew out a sigh and inventoried my fingers and toes. Each one was accounted for.

That was weird.

A soft whimper sounded from the dugout then. When I jogged close to it, I found a blue-eyed Siberian husky puppy with a Cracker Jack box stuck on his nose lying on the bench. He looked in my direction, pawed at his captor, his head lowered, inching forward. His eyes caught mine.

"Okay. But if you bite me, I bite back." I was taking no chances after the rat dog incident.

The candy box slipped off after the third tug, and old blue eyes licked my cheek. He toppled from the brick dugout and chased after the music.

Well, that was interesting.

Then I heard screeches mixed with cries of joy coming from the park.

My stomach did a little flip-flop. Something was wrong.

Slowly I emerged from the dugout.

Dozens of dogs were tramping out of the woods, jumping over one another. Terriers, bulldogs, Labradors, mutts, golden retrievers, Dobermans, and off in the distance, one Irish wolfhound that stared at me for an instant before he darted in the opposite direction.

I was pretty pleased that the spell had worked. Well, technically. With one minor flaw.

From the looks of it, I had called every lost dog in a thirty-mile radius. And possibly a thirty-year lifespan.

But there was only one I cared about.

Somehow, he seemed bigger, even though he was in the shadow of the trees. Perhaps it was the look on his face that made him appear authoritative. I swear he would have rolled his eyes at me if he could.

Or he may have seemed taller because of the new friend crouched next to him.

Chapter 4

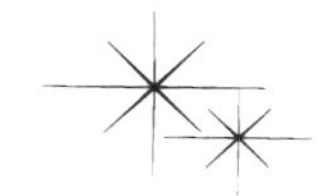

"If you pick up a starving dog and make him prosperous, he will not bite you; that is the principal difference between a dog and a man."

—Mark Twain

She was a long-haired beauty with angular features so sculpted she could have been molded out of clay. Her ears pointed to the sky and her face was traced with a golden tuft of hair that arranged itself into a heart down her narrow nose. The white fur on her chest puffed out around her as if by brush strokes, and I noticed as she lowered her head that she was trembling ever so slightly.

I gave a wide berth to the dogs emerging from the forest and started toward the edge of the tree line where Thor sat with the collie.

Voices cried out all around me. Exclamations of joy, disbelief, surprise, even anger as one kid screamed, "You told me Thumper was on a farm" to an apparently mortified set of parents.

I was still several yards away, but from the collie's demeanor it was obvious something was wrong. Was she hurt? Or just scared?

A flustered chief of police halted my opportunity to find out at that moment.

"Stacy, did you find Thor?"

I quickly signaled to Thor to lie down and his head ducked behind the weeds. Something about the way he was hovering around the collie made me think that Thor had a good reason for protecting her, and I didn't want her mixed up in the roundup of all the other dogs.

"Hey, Leo. I was just looking for him." I whistled. "Here, Thor, here, boy."

That goddamn Chihuahua ran over, baring his teeth at me. He shredded my shoelace before Leo commanded him to sit. He did, still training an eye on me.

It was as if he held a personal grudge.

He lifted a paw toward Leo, and the man bent down to check the dog's tag. He glanced up at me. "It says his name is Thor."

"Oh, that is just wrong."

The Chihuahua snapped in my direction—spit, actually—then licked Leo's hand lovingly.

Leo eyed me with suspicion. "I am not going to ask, because I don't want to know."

"What?"

He cocked his head toward the little shit, then back at me.

It took me a full twenty seconds to board his train of thought. When I did, I thought I would burst a lung laughing so hard.

"Do you mean to tell me that you think..." I pointed to the Chihuahua who was snuggling up to Leo, "that I would turn my dog into Scrappy-Doo?" I cackled. "Leo, even if I had that kind of power—which I do not—I wouldn't make him a misogynist."

Scrappy barked and lunged.

I didn't cower this time. "Well, you are! You have issues, pal." I stepped forward, but Leo put his hand between us.

"Okay, that's enough there, Dog Whisperer."

"He started it!" I whined.

Yes, I realize that arguing with an animal is not only stupid, but batshit crazy. My only defense was that this mutt hated me for no apparent reason when he should have been thanking me. I guess I was hurt. By a dog I just met.

I never said *I* didn't have issues.

Luckily, Gus interrupted before Leo pressed for further explanation.

"Hey, Stacy; hey, Chief. We need you over here. Animal control is on the way, but it looks like some of these dogs belong to folks here. If you give the okay, we can probably just release them to their owners."

Leo looked to be a little bit in shock as he watched the crowd weave around the dogs, some petting old friends, some playing fetch, some looking as astounded as the chief.

"Okay, well, duty calls." Leo smiled at me. "I'm sure you'll find Thor."

Scrappy growled, pointedly glared at me, and hopped around Leo like a circus dog.

"Seriously, what the hell did I do to you?" I asked the Chihuahua.

He backed up and peed on my ankle.

All I could do was look down, mouth agape.

Leo frowned and handed me a handkerchief. "Come on, little guy." They both sauntered off toward the band.

"This is not over!" I yelled.

I swear I wasn't going to take it personally until he lifted his leg.

I started back toward (the real) Thor, working on a second wind, smelling like a urinal. I quickly wiped my leg dry and tossed the cloth in a nearby garbage can. My phone was in my back pocket so I texted Chance and told him where to find me.

My pooch occupied the same spot as before except he was lying down, the collie resting her head on his backside. Thor was alert, waiting patiently for me to navigate the rocks, brambles, and milkweed covering the bank of the small creek that washed into the lake.

His new friend looked world-weary, not even bothering to lift her head even as twigs snapped and popped beneath my feet.

I wondered what had happened to her. Why hadn't she, along with all the other dogs, run from the woods in search of her family?

Finally I reached them. Thor glanced backward once and I took that as a sign to check on the beautiful creature resting beside him.

Her eyes were open, but listless, her breath shallow. She seemed not to care that I was in her space, but I passed my hand beneath her snout anyway. Her nose twitched and her eyes swung my way, then off in the distance.

My experience with dogs was limited to Thor, who pretty much took care of himself. However, I could tell that she was sick or injured, and I didn't want to make it worse by examining her with amateur hands.

Beyond the creek's edge, Chance called my name.

I popped up, waved a hand, and said, "Here."

He smiled, looking confused, the backpack loose in his hand. "Midnight dip?"

If only we could. "Not quite. Come down here."

Chance was much steadier on his feet than I was and he made his way over to the three of us in no time.

His forehead crinkled into concern. "Who's this?" He knelt beside me.

"I don't know. She doesn't have a collar. Do you recognize her?"

Chance sat on his heels, studying the fluffy dog. "I don't know anyone who has a collie. How do you know it's a female?"

Hmm. There was no answer to that. It was impossible to tell from her position on the ground.

"I just…know." I passed my hand beneath her nose again and gently stroked her cheek. Her eyes slid closed.

"Is she hurt?"

"I think so. I was afraid to touch her."

Chance chewed his bottom lip. "Well, the vet is closed at this hour and the closest emergency hospital is in Madison."

Madison, Wisconsin, was an hour and a half away. There was no way to tell what, if anything, was even wrong with the dog. I saw no blood, and she wasn't whimpering or even cringing. She just looked…exhausted.

"Oh, wait a minute." Chance snapped his fingers. "Dr. Zimmerman is out of town until Monday. His mother is having foot surgery this weekend so he asked me to stop by and take a look at securing his porch."

"Well, I'm sure there's someone taking his patients."

Chance smirked. "Yes, Doug Kessler. The kid usually works on my crew in the summer, but he's interning for Zimmerman."

"Can you call him?" An intern had to be better than nothing.

"Well, I could, but I just saw him down two beer bongs before all hell broke loose and now he's helping Leo sort out the canine invasion." Chance raised his eyebrows. "You wouldn't know anything about that, would you?"

"I was just looking for Thor." I circled around to my familiar. "Well, big guy, what do you think? Looks like there's only one option."

Thor swung his head around and the collie lifted hers. He trilled softly and flopped his tail a few times.

The sweet girl blinked her big lashes at Thor and put a paw on his hip. Prompted, she hoisted herself up and faced me.

Chance and I exchanged glances.

I took two steps back and said, "Come."

The collie perked her ears forward, but stayed put as Thor rose to his full height. He lowered his snout and nudged her gently.

She took three seemingly painless steps toward me.

I said to Chance, "She isn't limping. That's good."

I told her to sit and she did. A quick check beneath piles of fur didn't reveal any lacerations or a collar so I asked Chance to bring the truck around to the curb closest to the trees.

After he was gone, I knelt in front of Thor, patting his concrete shoulder.

"Good job, boy. We'll fix her right up."

Thor threw back his head and bayed. Then he leaned in and gave my ear a quick nibble.

The collie cocked her head at me, her eyes like dull marbles that had once shone.

"What happened to you, sweetheart?"

In a way, I was glad Doc Zimmerman was out of town. This little girl needed far more serious care than any veterinarian could offer.

Chapter 5

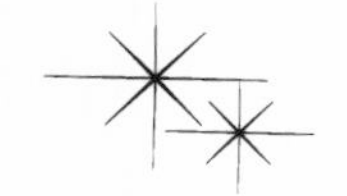

"Outside of a dog, a book is a man's best friend. Inside of a dog it's too dark to read."

—Groucho Marx

The Queen Anne house was dark when we pulled into the driveway at eleven o'clock. One porch light was lit, casting shadows across the lawn, and there were a few solar lights planted in the garden, but no illumination came from inside the old painted lady. She had been in my family for well over a hundred years. Maegan's husband, Birdie's father, built it with his own hands. His name escaped me now as an image of a silver-haired woman rocking on the porch infiltrated my mind.

Was that me in sixty years?

"Are you sure this is a good idea?" Chance asked, bursting my vision. "Don't they have to get up early to make breakfast for the guests?"

I nodded. There were three cars in the lot, which meant the Geraghty guesthouse was full to capacity. Although this time of year most bed-and-breakfasts throughout our small tourist town were booked on the weekends.

"What else can I do? Something's wrong with her, and Fiona is the only one who may be able to help at this hour. Besides"—I thumbed toward the backseat where Thor was gallantly scrunched up in a corner, flappy jowls smashed against the rear window just so his new friend could nap comfortably—"I have no idea if *she* is intact but I know *he* is. I really don't think it's a smart idea to let Casanova bunk with Sleeping Beauty."

"You're mixing metaphors."

"I'm exhausted."

Chance ran a large hand through his sandy locks. "Okay, I'll take Thor to the cottage and wait for you. Is that the plan?"

"Yep." I twined my arms around his neck and brought his head to mine for a kiss I hoped held more meaning than I was able to show at the moment. I leaned back and searched his eyes. There were no shadows there, just raw emotion.

"You're welcome, angel," he said.

"You really need to come up with a new term of endearment."

"I've been working on it."

Chance got out of the car and lifted the patient off the backseat, setting her on the ground gently. She yawned, stretched, and waited for Thor to jump down. When he did, she began to follow him toward the cottage at the back of the property where I lived. The Dane stopped, turned, and made some sort of half groan, half yelp kind of noise and the collie halted.

I got out of the truck, grabbed my backpack, and approached her cautiously, both of us watching Chance and Thor make their way to the cottage. Thor glanced back once as he crossed the threshold, then trotted inside.

That was the first time the smaller dog made a sound. It was a quiet whimper, as if she had just watched hope walk out the door. The night was silent again except for the chirrup of crickets.

I reached for my crystal bag and fished until I found the rose quartz wand. Rose quartz is best known for love spells, but it's also a great stone for healing emotional turmoil and alleviating anxiety.

Tentatively I raised my left hand to the top of the dog's head and placed it there. She was shivering, her muscles taut. The wand loose in my right hand, I turned to face the collie and swept my left palm over her soft fur, imagining as I did all the toxic energy leaving her body. I followed the sweep with the wand pointed toward her tail and walked the length of her, finally shaking it out at the end of the pathway that led to the back door of the inn. I lifted my arm toward the moon to recharge the wand with positive, feminine vibrations and blew out all the air in my lungs.

That would have to do for now.

The brown-eyed girl was standing where I had left her, and this time, as I made my approach, her tail wagged just a bit. I gave her a big smile and went in search of the key to the back kitchen door of the Geraghty house.

I bent down to pry open the mouth of the gargoyle that housed the spare key when a light flickered on. Then off. Then on again.

The kitchen door was a horizontal number, with the bottom half made of solid wood and the top glass framed in wood. In front of that was the screen door. I peeked through the glass just as Fiona was reaching for the teapot. The light (which I identified as a night light) shone on, then off again.

Just in time for me to scare the living crap out of Fiona.

She jumped, but stifled her scream with both hands as soon as she recognized it was me. Since the kitchen was on the first floor, all the way at the back of the house, I was pretty sure her guests hadn't heard. Those rooms were up the stairs and toward the front of the home.

However, I wasn't sure if Birdie or Lolly had been startled awake.

Fiona rushed to unlock the back door and said, "Child, what on earth are you doing lurking around out there in the middle of the night?"

"Fiona, I'm sorry, I really need to talk to you. It's sort of an—" She flipped the switch for the sconce near the stove, and I was so stunned by her appearance, I couldn't speak for a moment.

Her skin was glowing—radiating almost—as if she hadn't seen a day past thirty-five. Her hair was rolled in pink cushion rollers protected by a silk scarf, but other than that, she looked like she was getting ready for a photo shoot.

I asked, "Do you always go to bed with your makeup on?"

"Is that what you came here to discuss? Beauty tips?"

"No, of course not, it's just—never mind. Why are you awake?"

Fiona left the door open for me to come inside and went back to the stove and her teapot. "It's the darndest thing." She opened the antique pie safe where they stored dried herbs. "I slept soundly for a few hours and then just bolted right out of bed." She shook her head, mumbling about chamomile and lavender.

She knew, albeit subconsciously, but she knew. They must have called to her. The dogs from the woods must have panicked and sought out a guide. Is that why she seemed even younger and healthier than usual? Did she somehow gather strength from the animal kingdom?

I held the door open for the collie. She gingerly stepped onto the cold tile and sat near me. "I think I may know why, Auntie."

Fiona paused, her back to me. She cocked her head to the side and then slowly turned around, a wide smile tugging at her lips.

Her eyes fell to our houseguest. "And who have we here?"

The collie wasn't shy around my great-aunt. The dainty thing just pranced right up to her, welcoming a pat.

Perhaps now is as good a time as any to explain why I came to Fiona for help with this damaged dog.

You see, all the Geraghty gifts are acquired, not taught. Sure, we've been schooled on herbal craft, spellcasting, recipes, even exercises for enhancing intuition. But true knowledge is gained only through experience, and Geraghty gifts are, in a way, *earned.*

Kind of like those merit badges they pass out to Girl Scouts, although rather than helping a disabled person cross the street, a Geraghty might just teleport him. If she had the ability.

Anyway, Fiona's magic has always been matchmaking and love spells, but her passion—her "other calling," if you will—was not discovered until she met her third and favorite husband, Patrick Edward Burns, DVM.

Dr. Burns walked into Fiona's life right around the time she, like all Geraghty women, came into her true power at the threshold age of thirty.

The good doctor had just opened up shop in town, fresh out of vet school. The story goes that he was on his way to Chicago from Iowa, where his family lived, when he spotted an injured dog on the side of the road. The town had no clinic at the time, so he did the best he could patching up the dog's broken leg with the supplies on hand and drove the animal to the nearest facility—fifty miles away. He decided then that he might be more useful in a small hamlet than a big city.

That's when Fiona found herself with an ill Siamese kitten that belonged to an out-of-town friend.

"The little darling was a descendent of the familiar Mother brought home for me when I was still in the cradle," she once told me. "That was before she knew my gift. Not all witches require familiars, but most start out with one. However, in my case they come as needed, so being attached to just one, well, that hindered my development."

Fiona had embraced her gift right from the get-go and, unlike myself, never wavered from it.

"Your grandmother's talent to heal works only on people, not animals. Therefore, I loaded the kitten into the car and drove him to the new veterinarian," she had said. "He took my breath away the moment I laid eyes on him.

He was movie-star handsome and quite charming—like Cary Grant!"

Dr. Burns couldn't find a thing wrong with the kitten, who perked right up on the exam table, chasing the penlight and pawing at the stethoscope around the vet's neck. Burns couldn't find a thing wrong with Fiona either. He asked her to dinner that day and they were married six weeks later.

Soon Fiona found herself working at the vet's office, and she discovered a talent for healing pets in ways a doctor of medicine could not. You see, love comes in many forms, and while Fiona's talent was romantic love, she also had a knack for healing soured friendships, spoiled partnerships, and broken families. (Why she was not able to reconcile Birdie with my grandfather, I'll never understand.) So when animals came to the clinic with symptoms not relating to any affliction he could find, Burns trusted Fiona to heal their inner aches and pains—broken hearts and wounded souls. To hear anyone tell it, they were quite the team.

As I stood now in the Geraghty Girls' kitchen, beneath the dim light of the toleware wall sconce, I thought how tragic it would be to lose a true soul mate.

Fiona had already run her hands over the collie whose name, she informed me, was Keesha. I explained how Thor had found her in the woods and that she seemed lethargic, omitting my role in drawing her, and dozens of other canines, to me via a botched spell. I figured she'd hear all about it tomorrow and I wasn't in the mood for a lecture on living up to my potential.

Fiona said, "Nothing feels broken. No pain anywhere that she wants me to know about right now."

Her eyes never left Keesha as she relayed this information to me. I was mesmerized, watching her work her gift, and I wondered if I would ever have that much faith, that much trust in myself even.

"Stacy?"

I rushed over to the apothecary table. Usually it was the center island of the kitchen, but now it served as a makeshift exam table with a bright bulb hovering above it. It smelled faintly of rosemary and lemon. "Yes?"

Fiona gave me a stern look. "Stop fidgeting. All that knee bouncing and nail biting is frightening this poor creature."

Keesha gave me a forlorn look and I apologized.

"Dear, top drawer next to the sink, please fetch my reading glasses, and there should be a small flashlight. I'll need that as well."

I retrieved the items and handed them to Fiona.

She slipped the glasses onto her nose and lifted Keesha's lips. "Gums are pink." She flashed a light in both perky ears. "No mites." She held each eyelid open and flashed the light across the dog's pupils. "No sign of cataracts, or corneal disease. I'd say she's rather young. Three, maybe four years old."

"Can you tell if she's been spayed?"

Fiona gently coaxed Keesha to lie on the table. She lifted her leg and filtered through the mass of wavy fur that covered the animal's belly.

"No scar that I can see, no tattoo either, which is common today. Her stomach is fairly taut." She lowered the collie's leg and Keesha stood up, panting.

Fiona removed her glasses. "My guess is no, but you would need an ultrasound to be certain."

She crossed to the sink and turned on the faucet to wash her hands. Keesha let out a sharp bark and sat on the table.

"How about a midnight snack?" Fiona asked, and Keesha raised both front paws and scratched at the air.

Fiona smiled and filled a ceramic mixing bowl with bottled water. "Presently, what she needs is sustenance and a good night's sleep." She set the water on the floor and I lifted the collie from the table. She lapped at the refreshment heartily.

"I'll do some work on her in the morning." Fiona was sifting through the cabinets, finally settling on some plain saltine crackers. She tossed a few to Keesha who caught them one by one. She seemed livelier already. "Come back around noon and we'll discuss my findings."

My great-aunt was at the back steps, poised to turn the island light off when I said, "Will you keep her here until we find out who her family is? With Thor, I mean, you know..."

Fiona chuckled and shook her head. "That, my dear niece, depends on your grandmother." She floated up the back stairs, her robe waving behind her, the soft click of dog nails echoing her steps.

I let myself out and jogged the few feet to my cottage, taking one long, last look at the moon. This time of year, at its fullest, pagans refer to it as the Mead Moon because of all the honey wine they prepare in anticipation of the solstice celebration, or Litha—the longest and strongest sun day of the year. Hence the term honeymoon for those after-wedding trips that take place in June.

I took a few calming breaths, releasing the stress of the day. Exhaustion was settling deeper into my bones, but the alcohol was wearing off.

As I gazed upward, right before my eyes, the iridescent ball of light in the sky transformed into the giant head of a white tiger. It blinked its turquoise eyes just once.

Then it was gone.

Chapter 6

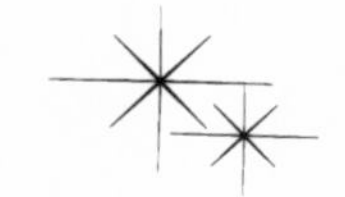

"The great pleasure of a dog is that you may make a fool of yourself with him and not only will he not scold you, but he will make a fool of himself too."

—Samuel Butler

When you've tossed and turned in bed all night because someone was hogging the covers, the pillows, and the entire mattress, the best way to wake up is alone and with the aroma of bacon sizzling on the stove.

Plus coffee. Lots and lots of coffee.

Unfortunately, that wasn't what happened this Sunday morning.

"Son of an assjacket," I mumbled. "Please get off me." His shoulder was smothering my face and his position led me to believe that I was functioning as a teddy bear.

He rolled over, kicking my stomach in the process, and let out a fart that could clear a morgue.

"Jesus, Moses, and Frank!" I fanned the covers like a maniac, on the verge of kicking him back when Chance ducked his head into my bedroom.

"What's wrong?" He was wearing a pair of sweats and a short white apron with nothing else north of the navel.

Thor was still sprawled across the bed, snoring happily and drooling all over my pillow.

"I just hate being woken up in the middle of a headlock. It's unnerving." I slipped out of bed and reached for my purple silk robe.

"Who is Frank?"

"You know, Frank. The apostle." I stuffed my feet in fuzzy slippers and faced him.

He was biting his bottom lip.

"What?"

"I don't think there was an apostle named Frank."

"Are you sure?"

He nodded. "Pretty much."

"Dammit, Birdie," I grumbled and made my way into the bathroom.

I hated it when she played tricks like that. For some reason, she found it amusing to feed me false information about any religion but her own.

This one was going on my payback list.

I did my business and washed up. The cottage had an open floor plan, with the living room, bathroom, and kitchen all spilling into each other. Chance was at the counter pouring two glasses of orange juice when I opened the bathroom door. The muscles in his back flexed with the flow of his arm movements, his skin sun-kissed from working outdoors. It was a yummy sight that only enhanced the sugary scent of maple syrup and rich butter melting in a pan.

"You hungry?" Chance asked. "I'm making French toast."

"Sounds wonderful." I circled around and kissed his shoulder, and then I poured myself a cup of coffee and plopped on a stool at the breakfast bar. There was a pillow and a neatly folded blanket on the sofa cushion.

"Did you sleep in the living room?" I asked.

Chance whisked milk and eggs together. He nodded as he reached for the spice rack above the stove. "I tried to get Thor off the bed, but when he's that tired, there's no point in arguing with him and I certainly wasn't going to force the issue." He sprinkled some cinnamon into the batter, whisked again, and sliced off four pieces of Lolly's homemade sweet bread. "You need a bigger bed." He winked.

"Maybe I'll just get Thor his own." I wondered if he would need a queen like mine. I also wondered where I would put it in my one-bedroom home. "I promised I'd take him swimming today. Do you want to come?" I took a sip of my coffee. Delicious.

"Sorry, babe, I have a couple of jobs to bid this morning."

"On a Sunday?"

Chance flipped the French toast, which smelled divine. "No such thing as a lazy summer for a good contractor." He smiled at me as he slid a plate of perfectly crafted carbohydrates in front of me. "Besides, you've worked many a Sunday."

That was true. I helped out at the inn whenever I was needed, but no one asked me to do that this weekend, so I was on furlough. Perhaps the house wasn't full after all or perhaps it was a group of repeat customers, who are often easier to service.

Chance said, "How about dinner?"

I smiled back at him and reached for a napkin and a fork. "Sounds great. My place?"

"Nah, why don't we go out and get pampered?"

"Deal." We clicked our juice glasses together and Thor announced that he was ready to rise by bellowing out a wide-mouthed yawn and shaking the bedroom floor with his weight.

A cardinal's song wafted through the screen door and Thor sauntered over to watch the little red bird as he fluttered into a nearby spruce tree that sat between the cottage and the main house. Thor looked rather annoyed that such a tiny creature could make all that racket. The dog bowed, sticking his huge ass in the air, then followed through to up-dog, stretching his chest to capacity. Ready to reclaim the tree the cardinal was about to call home, Thor raised a meaty paw to the latch and slapped the door open.

Chance watched as he trotted off the porch. "Not really a morning guy, is he?"

"Neither was Cinnamon." My cousin was Thor's original person before I moved back to town from Chicago. Thor decided that was an error that needed rectifying. He'd lived with me ever since.

I thanked Chance for the meal and dug into my French toast, savoring every bite.

After breakfast, I cleaned up the dishes and kissed Chance good-bye. We agreed that I would make the restaurant reservations when Thor and I returned from swimming.

When he heard the word *swimming*, Thor pranced around the yard like a new puppy, barking and yipping at the air. I coaxed him inside, put my hair up, slipped into a swimsuit, and packed us a bag full of towels, water, and peanut butter dog treats. Thor disappeared into the bedroom to search for his rubber octopus. His favorite water toy.

It was still early. The heat hadn't quite settled over the town yet as I loaded Thor and the bag into the backseat of my SUV. We could have walked there, because it was just on the other side of town, but with all the excitement yesterday and as heavy as my pooch slept last night, I feared that a long walk coupled with an exhilarating swim might result in a dog too tired to make the trip home. And it was no fun trying to push Thor back up that steep hill when he didn't want to go, believe me. He's been known to hitchhike home.

I slid my sunglasses over my nose and drove the few blocks to the conservation area that led to the lake. There's a dead-end street nearby where I like to park for easy access to the trail. I pulled into a slot, clipped a leash on Thor, and grabbed our stuff. The quietest part of the lake was on the opposite side from where the festival had taken place the night before. This area had a single picnic table with a small patch of beach that was a bit rocky, a bit overgrown with weeds, but where a Great Dane could dig, splash, and frolic without obliterating a sandcastle or sending a rip current over a ten-year-old's head.

I removed Thor's leash and tossed it on the table. As I fished inside the bag for a bottle of water, Thor stuck his head inside to find "Octi." He emerged with it, tossing the thing in the air, and squeaking the life out of it. Luckily the water bottle suffered minimal slobber.

"Hang on, buddy. Let me take off my cover-up first." I kicked away my flip-flops and removed the purple terry cloth sundress, setting it on top of the bag.

Then I forgot all about my parents, the tiger, the collie, even the clown, and just had a riotous time with my best pal.

We played catch and tag for a couple of hours before it was time for a break. I tossed Thor some of his cookies, poured fresh water into his portable bowl, and grabbed a bottle for myself.

The sun was high in the sky by that time so we sprawled out on the sand and relaxed for a bit, enjoying the quiet symphony of twittering birds, croaking frogs, and musical insects. Thor took an interest in an army of ants that were transporting supplies back to their troops, while I pulled out my Kindle and settled into a good murder mystery.

I got through four chapters before Thor charged into the lake again after an unsuspecting dragonfly. The sweat was pouring off me and I decided to take a dip too. I walked out into the lake, enchanted by a crane that must have swooped in from the Mississippi. She stood on an outer bank, gobbling bugs and pecking at berries, her impossibly thin legs balanced on a log. I waded out farther into the lake, squishing my toes into the wet sand before I finally felt a mucky cold sludge where the sand dropped off and the basin was deeper. I did a few far-reaching breaststrokes when I heard a sharp squawk. I looked back to find the crane twisting her neck, cawing and calling when—to my complete astonishment—her delicate beak bulged, her legs swelled, and her body stretched and rippled until it finally morphed into the white tiger from the tree.

She took a few steps toward the lake, her body gracefully navigating the thick brush, flattening cattails and phlox with her thick paws. Then a few more steps. Then a few more. Soon she was standing on top of the water, her reflection casting a mirror image across the glassy surface.

I blinked, cartoon style.

White tigers represent focus, courage, and strength. They are considered "sisters of the moon," able to harness lunar magic and other feminine energies.

Which was why I was shocked by her presence in the daylight.

Well, that and the fact that they are not native to this area, or, to my knowledge, possess the ability to float on water.

She lowered her mighty head, her eyes trained on me, and I nearly peed my suit. My arms started shaking as I tried to conjure up the lesson she was here to teach before she got any closer.

Think, Stacy.

Tigers were associated with water. Good swimmers. Devoted mothers. They had stamina, patience, and strength. Power. They were messengers of, of...what? Was it adventure? Yes, that, but...something else too.

And then it hit me.

Truth. Danger.

Uh-oh.

I twirled around, a complete 360-degree turn, the water lapping over my shoulders, my eyes darting every which way.

The trees were still, save for a slight rustling from a summer breeze. No movement across the way either. The lake was calm. No boats. No swimmers. No hockey-masked men with chain saws.

But I felt it in my gut. The nausea came in a rush, and a lesson that Birdie had been drilling into my head for years echoed in my mind. *Always be on guard, always heed the warnings your body and the spirit guides are trying to tell you.*

Harmful intent.

I took a deep breath to calm myself, then backstroked toward the beach, keeping my eyes open for anything out of the ordinary.

Off the left bank, Thor was digging a hole in the sand, oblivious to the tiger and to my panic.

Another deep breath.

If Thor wasn't concerned, that was a good sign. Very good, because it surely meant that if he didn't sense danger, it wasn't going to happen now. The tiger was just telling me that something ominous loomed and that I needed to prepare.

I set my gaze on her, hoping to signal that I understood and to thank her for the warning.

Her sea foam eyes darkened, her pink nose twitched. She cocked her head as if to say, "I tried to tell you."

And then I was plunged into the belly of the lake.

Chapter 7

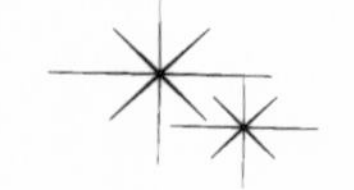

Struggling to stay focused, remain calm, and hold your breath all at the same time when something or someone is clamped onto your foot and dragging you to a watery grave is not easy.

I kicked and fought, thrashed in the water, but the force, or weight, or whatever had a grip on me was powerful.

And two thoughts occurred to me.

The first was: *My father was murdered.*

The second was: *Now it's my turn.*

I couldn't see anything below me, so I focused on the ray of light penetrating the surface and pushed my arms up and away, up and away, up and away. I kicked and kicked, trying to dislodge myself from the force that was binding me, but the more I bucked, the harder I fought, the farther I sank into the cold, murky depths of the lake I once loved.

This was it. This was how I was going to die. I would never know what happened to my father. Never see my mother again. Never get married, have babies, or take a trip to Home Depot.

I had failed both my past and future families.

My strength was waning, my breath was running out, but I had just enough energy for one final battle.

I doubled over, thumping at my own ankle, feeling only flesh, but still unable to see my attacker. I twisted in the water. Spiraling and spinning, reaching my arms far over my head to gain leverage and pull myself from this black hole.

That's when my second foot was captured.

I was pulled down deep enough that my ears popped, my head exploded with pain, and I lost consciousness.

Chapter 8

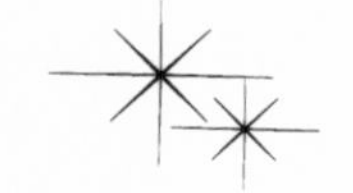

"All his life he tried to be a good person. Many times, however, he failed. For after all, he was only human. He wasn't a dog."

—Charles M. Schulz

When I opened my eyes again, I wondered if I was dead.

If I was dead, why was no one there to guide me into the Summerland? Where were my ancestors who had gone before me? Maegan? Dad?

If I wasn't dead, how the hell was I still able to breathe underwater?

The answers came not in a bright white light full of love and acceptance and fluttering angel wings like you see in the movies.

It came in the form of a sucker punch.

There were hands on my waist, and the face in front of me looked concerned at first. I blinked, and the man who was holding onto me lifted a finger. No wait, two fingers.

He flashed a peace sign.

I was frozen in fear and because the water was numbingly cold, but I nodded anyway, because really, what choice was there?

And I realized I could actually breathe just fine. I didn't dwell on that because there were more pressing matters at hand. Like how do I get back to land? And who was this guy?

He pointed down.

That was when I saw the concrete block chained to his leg.

Instinctively, I dove down to see if I could free him, but he grabbed my ankle, flipped me over, and shook his head.

He held my gaze for a split second. He was wearing a red plaid shirt over a white tank top and jeans that probably didn't look much better dry. His neck was like a Roman column and his eyes were filled with broken promises swimming in regret.

In a flash, he transformed into a rotting corpse with hollow sockets and a gaping mouth. Every orifice had creepy-crawlies slithering in and out of it.

I freaked the hell out.

My arms took on a life of their own, flailing in directions I didn't know they could move. My legs became ninja warriors, writhing at anything and everything they could hit.

Must Get Away from the Lake Monster.

I just knew his plan was to make me his soggy bride. Or maybe he was some sort of water zombie and I was his next meal.

He slugged me again. Really hard.

Holy nutfugget, that hurt!

I whacked him right back in his doughy face, which had returned to its original shape of Normal-Looking Human.

His head bobbed, but he still held fast to me. I was grateful for the small fact that at least now he looked like a roofer after a long day rather than a Wes Craven creation.

He made the peace sign again and I think he tried to roll his eyes, but I couldn't be sure.

He pointed down once more.

I trailed his finger with my gaze. While I was somehow able to see shapes, movement, and hints of light, there was nothing I could pinpoint that seemed important. Some algae, water creatures, broken beer bottles, and an old boot.

I shrugged.

He got agitated then and started pointing down with both hands, frantically.

When he let me go, all the air left my lungs.

Quickly, he grabbed me again and I was able to breathe.

I understood at that moment that he was doing it. He was responsible for my breath, my ability to see into these dark depths. He was keeping me alive.

I felt a little better about our relationship after that and decided that whatever task the dead guy wanted me to fulfill, I better do it soon or I might never get out of here. Plus, I was getting really tired of being slapped.

I concentrated one last time, carefully scanning the lake bed.

Several feet away from the concrete block, something gleamed. Almost like moonlight, it had an iridescent quality.

I pointed in that direction and he nodded enthusiastically. Then he grabbed my feet and pushed me forward.

The glowing object would have been out of his reach, what with being anchored to the block and all, but using me as leverage, like you might a wooden spoon to reach something under the stove, worked like a charm.

From the mushy floor of the lake, I pulled out a pearl-faced wristwatch.

We floated up a few feet together and I offered it to him. He shook his head. Then pointed from himself to me.

And in another split second, I was catapulted back up to the surface like a human cannonball.

I sucked in all the fresh air I could, thankful to be back above the water. There was no telling how long I had been down there. Minutes? Hours?

A quick scan of the perimeter revealed Thor still digging in the same spot as if I had never left. Which, technically, I guess I hadn't.

I dragged myself back to the beach and collapsed on my extra-large towel. It was still a bit damp and the sun was in the same spot in the sky.

As if time had stood still.

I took a minute to examine it. It looked to be mostly stainless steel besides the face, with more buttons than I would ever need in a timepiece. It was in good shape, minus a bit of sea scum that I wiped away with a towel. The second hand ticked by, so it seemed to be functioning just fine.

There was one bottle of water left in my bag. I carefully stuffed the watch in the plastic baggie I used to protect my Kindle, put it in a side compartment, and zipped it shut. I grabbed the water and drank half, thinking about my "gift."

The first memory I had of communicating with the deceased was when I was five years old. I was in the garden trying to catch a butterfly with a fly swatter. It seemed like the most efficient method at the time, and since I hadn't yet learned about death and dying, why not use brute force?

Not the shiniest penny in the wishing well, you might say.

Anyway, I was smacking at this lovely yellow-and-black beauty, hitting only air, when Mrs. Krenshaw, my preschool teacher, happened to be walking through the yard.

She knelt down to my level and held out her arms as if she were dancing to music I couldn't hear. She smiled at me, a warm, loving smile, and the gorgeous butterfly landed right on her nose. She gestured to me to try to do the same and I did, although the fluttering creature was keeping its distance from me by that time.

We spent a few more minutes in the garden, me chattering away about school and the friends I was making, and Mrs. Krenshaw simply nodding and smiling. When my mother interrupted to explain that my teacher was ill and she wouldn't be in class tomorrow, I started to protest. Until I looked back at Mrs. Krenshaw who smiled bravely, waved, and walked right through the gate.

When I relayed the story, Birdie and the aunts were terribly excited that my gift was gaining power. My mother was torn, I think, although she didn't dissuade the lessons they taught me at that time.

Today, I'd learned a new lesson.

So far, I had not been able to hear the spoken words of the departed. The messages from spirits came in the form of dreams, visions, or objects, but I wasn't capable of conversing with them directly. At least not in the traditional sense. Perhaps through a scrying session, I might catch a glimpse of a conversation between a dead person and a living individual.

At times, I hear Maegan's voice—or what I perceive to be my great-grandmother's voice—in my head, but only via words she had written in the Blessed Book.

What just happened was different. It was desperate. This man—either a suicide or homicide victim—wanted someone to find that watch badly enough that, rather than move on to the Summerland, he waited in that dark abyss until someone came along.

Until I came along.

But why? What was so important about it?

And what—if anything—did it have to do with me?

I stood. I needed to do two things. The first was to call the police station and somehow report the body at the bottom of Eagle Lake without explaining how I knew it was there.

The second was to make sure the deceased moved forward on his journey. As the Seeker of Justice, it was my job to ensure that the dead who came to me find their way to their next destination.

A task I was not looking forward to after my encounter with this particular member of the nonliving.

I shivered.

Birdie always said the dead could never hurt you.

But I learned today that they can touch you.

If they can touch you, wouldn't that mean they can hurt you?

Chapter 9

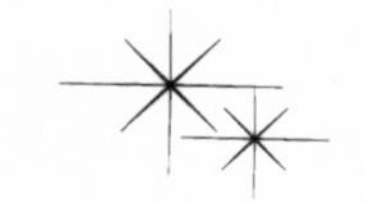

A new dispatcher answered the call. She sounded a lot younger and much more enthusiastic than the previous woman who had worked there. There was no need to clog up the nine-one-one system since the body wasn't getting any deader, so I called the station direct.

"Amethyst Police Department. This is Amy. What can I help you with?"

"Hi, Amy, my name is Stacy Justice and—"

"Did you say Stacy Justice?"

"I did. Listen, I—"

"Stacy Justice the reporter?"

"Yes, that's right. The reason I'm calling—"

"Hang on."

I heard some papers shuffling around.

"All right, I'm back. Go ahead…oh, damn."

"What? What's wrong?"

The woman sighed. "I had August in the pool."

"Excuse me?"

"You're calling about a dead body, right?"

"How did you know that?"

"Lucky guess. Damn, Gus won."

"Won what? What are you talking about?"

"Well, they hired me in May after I graduated and there was this pool going on to see when you would find a dead body. I had August. Gus had June."

I was speechless. For like a nanosecond. "Isn't that illegal?"

"Gee, I don't know, is it?"

This wasn't going well.

"Amy, please put someone on the phone who has a badge."

"Okeydoke."

A few seconds later, Leo asked, "You found another one? That has to be a record."

"I haven't found a dead body in months, okay? Cut me some slack."

"Are you absolutely sure it's a dead person? It's not a mannequin or anything?"

I sighed. "What month did you have?"

"October."

"Wow, that long. I appreciate your faith."

"Where are you?"

I told him where I was, that I was safe, and that Thor had trudged the body up but it sank back down. I also said I would wait so I could point them in the right direction. The concrete block never came up.

I could tell from his tone that he didn't buy the story, but he didn't press it either. When I hung up, my dog was standing in front of me, carrying something.

I held out my hand and he deposited a cell phone into it. It was a cheaper model, a flip phone.

A good deal of sand caked the cracks and crevices, and only a few teeth marks marred the edges.

Could this have belonged to the man in the lake?

If it did, it was evidence, and since I had no intention of handing over the watch until I figured out if the floater wanted *me* specifically to find it or just anyone, I figured that withholding any more evidence would be an even more serious crime.

Rationalizing behavior that authorities may construe as poor judgment is another Geraghty trait. One I was getting better at every day I lived here.

Not that I was proud of it.

A few minutes later, Leo and Gus came through the tree line.

"Why couldn't we bring him, Chief? You know he doesn't like to be away from you."

Leo muttered, "Not now, Gus."

"Who?" I asked.

"He's such a cute little thing, Stacy."

"Gus," Leo warned.

"What, Stacy likes dogs." Gus was talking and moving like a man with way too much caffeine in his system. "You know how all them dogs came running around the park yesterday? Well, most of them had owners who lived right in town, but this little Chihuahua had nobody, see—"

I swung my head toward Leo. "You adopted that piranha? Are you kidding me?"

"He's a good dog."

"He tried to eat all four of my extremities," I said.

Leo laughed. "Yeah, he really doesn't like you. But he's great with everyone down at the station. I'm sure it was just a misunderstanding."

"Try explaining that to his next victim when he goes for the jugular."

"How about you explain why eight of the dogs recovered were considered deceased by the people who buried them?"

I swallowed hard. That wasn't good. How could that happen? Lost dogs, yes, but resurrected dogs? That was way too much. If Birdie found out I had screwed up that bad, she was going to kill me.

"Can we just get on with this, please? It's been a trying day." And my grandmother's sure to make it worse when she hears about my drunken, botched spell.

Gus flipped open a notebook and I explained where in the lake I saw the body, leaving out the part of momentarily turning into a mermaid. I listened as Leo told him who to call first for the dive and then I remembered the phone. I pointed them to that as well.

"Is that it? Can I go now?"

"Yes. I think we have everything we need. Are you going to cover the story?"

"I don't know." I stuffed my towel in the bag and slipped my cover-up on. "That's up to Parker. Come on, Thor." He came prancing up to me and I clipped the leash on him.

We were halfway up the bank when Leo called, "One more thing, Stacy."

I turned back.

"You look amazing in a bikini."

I pulled into the driveway at the inn and cut the engine. Thor's tail thumped in anticipation, and I decided it might be a good idea to have a chat with him. I swung my arm over the seat and turned to face the dog.

"All right, my friend, listen up."

Thor's ears tilted toward me.

"When we go inside, I want you on your best behavior, do you understand?"

He groaned and slapped a paw on the passenger headrest.

I narrowed my eyes. "I mean it. That girl in there is in pristine condition and she's going to stay that way until I can find her family. So that means"—I counted on my fingers—"no sniffing, no licking, no leg-lifting, no googly eyes, and—above all else—keep the lipstick in the tube. Comprendo?"

Thor slapped his other paw on the front seat, settled his chin between the pair, and looked at me with raised eyebrows.

"Good. Let's go."

I hopped out of the car, slung the bag over my shoulder, and circled around to open the rear door.

Thor decided I hadn't properly toweled him off at the beach so the second his paws hit the pavement, he shook his entire body forcefully, head to tail, launching a loogie at my chest.

I tried to wipe it away with my damp towel, but only managed to maximize the snot stain.

Thor sat down, waiting patiently.

"You did that on purpose, didn't you?"

He blinked, innocently.

I bent over, my face near his. "Let's not forget that you were the one who kicked Chance out of bed last night. Consider us even."

He snorted and trotted up the steps while I fished for a key. It was close to 11:30 when I twisted the door handle. I could still smell the freshly picked strawberries and mint from the garden. Lolly must have made her signature berry crisp.

Fiona had asked me to come by at noon, but rather than change clothes at my place first, I thought perhaps they needed help cleaning up the breakfast dishes. Plus, on Sundays, Thor was treated to a special feast, which was why I'd kept his breakfast light.

What I didn't expect was a Metallica song rushing at me, accompanied by a thin, heavily tattooed man who spent too much time in the sun and not enough time at the dentist.

"Oh, hey there, mama." He raised his chin. "Sup?" He punched a button on his phone and turned off the music.

"Nothing much. Sup with you?" I hung my bag on the hall hook.

The man, who looked to be past forty, was drinking what appeared to be a Bloody Mary and his hair was still wet from a shower. He was wearing biker boots and a muscle shirt that read *More Cowbell.* He tucked a chunk of hair behind his ear and said, "Just chillin'. Long night, you know. My ears are still ringing."

He smiled and lowered himself into a tufted pink chair adorned with ivory tassel trim and lace doilies. I couldn't help but think he would look less out of place if he were about to sit down to tea with Queen Elizabeth.

Then he crossed his legs and reached for a coaster, carefully arranging it on the end table before he placed the glass on top of it. He double-checked to make sure it was doing the job.

I glanced at Thor, who didn't know what to make of the guy. He paused, then gave the all clear by curling up on the cool tile in the hallway and closing his eyes. Only his nose moved, searching for a clue as to what was on today's menu.

"Awesome dog. Saw him last night. He yours?" The guy took a sip from his Bloody Mary, carefully lifting it and placing it back on the coaster.

"Yep, all mine. That's Thor."

The man smacked his head. "Geez, sorry, chica." He stood. "Where the hell are my manners? I'm Brian, but my friends and the band call me Buzz."

"Oh, you're in the band. You guys were great last night, really great," I said.

He smiled and thanked me. Asked if I was staying at the inn as well.

"No. Actually, I'm the granddaughter. I just came by to help out."

"Well, your grandmother sure knows how to put on a spread." He slapped his stomach. "I'm stuffed." He lifted his glass and said, "And I don't usually drink, especially not this early, but Lolly makes the best Bloody Marys." He took another sip.

"Well, it was great to meet you. I'm sure I'll see you around. By the way, I'm Stacy."

He stood and extended his hand.

A jolt surged through my body the instant I grasped it. Then the vision came. The man from the lake in the plaid shirt, yelling about something. A look of surprise on his face. Then a shocking blast of wet cold and...darkness.

The scream I had heard when I was playing in the outfield echoed in my head as the image faded.

"Hey, hey, Stacy. You all right?"

I realized I was gasping for air. I had to get out of there. Away from him. I backed up, slowly. "I'm fine. Just a little hot is all. I just need some water."

He took a step forward, looking confused, concerned. "Why don't you sit down? I'll get it."

"No!" I said too loudly. I smiled at him, trying to mask the nervousness. "I mean, it's fine, really. I just overdid it swimming is all."

I glanced at Thor. His legs were twitching. Asleep.

"Thanks, though. See you around." I fled.

It wasn't until I was halfway down the private hallway that I stopped and looked back.

Had I just grasped the hand of a killer?

Chapter 10

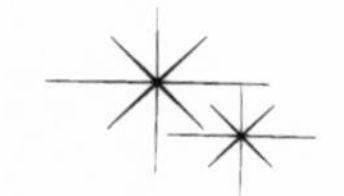

I gathered my composure and swung the door open to the kitchen. Fiona was standing at the sink, lemony suds popping all around her as her hands scrubbed a stubborn copper saucepan. Her auburn locks were twisted into a chignon and she wore a breezy linen blouse with matching pants. Espadrilles adorned her pedicured feet.

I heard the clinking of glasses and plates coming from the dining room, but I didn't see Birdie or Lolly.

"Hi, Aunt Fiona."

She had a smile on her face when she turned around, but it disappeared the moment she laid eyes on me.

"Heaven's, child, what happened to you? You look like you've been through a car wash without the car."

Yeah, fighting with a dead sea urchin will strip the shine right from your hair.

"I went swimming with Thor. I would have changed, but I wanted to see if you needed help cleaning up."

She rinsed the pan and set it in the drying rack and turned back to me. "Actually, we're all done here. Lolly is just putting away the dishes. Did you meet any of our guests?"

Should I mention what just happened? The visions that hit me when Brian touched me were intense. But what if I were wrong? What if the energy had just projected onto him somehow? He was at the park yesterday, after all. Perhaps he met the deceased?

Or maybe he was there when the cement block was chained to the dead man's ankle.

I decided to tread lightly. "I did meet one, yes. Brian. Said he was with the band. I was wondering when they had the chance to check in with having to play that late."

Fiona waved her hand. "Brian and his band, The Hell Hounds, have been staying here for years. I just gave him a key after the softball game." She grabbed a towel and began drying the saucepan. "They play at Cinnamon's tavern sometimes too."

At times, I felt like I had never left; other times it was as if I had been gone a million years. I had never heard of this band before and certainly had never seen them perform at the Black Opal. Cinnamon might be a better source of information than the aunts on this guy. It was one thing to be on your best behavior at a bed-and-breakfast run by three older ladies, but at a booze-fueled bar, people weren't as guarded.

I turned my attention to the initial reason for my visit. "How is Keesha? Did you learn more about her?"

Fiona was rummaging through the refrigerator. She pulled out some leftover pot roast and sweet potatoes, grabbed Thor's dish from the cupboard, and set it on the counter.

"Oh my, yes. She's quite the chatterbox, that one. She's resting comfortably."

She turned the oven to two hundred degrees and scooped the meat and potatoes into the bowl, then opened the freezer for a bag of green beans. She dumped that in the bowl as well and spooned some gravy on top. Then she put the whole thing in the oven.

"Why don't you just get a microwave?" I asked.

"Whatever for?"

She pulled out a stool and sat, looking tired and not nearly as youthful as she had the night before.

I fixed us each an iced tea and sat across from her.

"Thank you, sweetheart."

"Are you all right?"

Her eyes sparkled like emeralds in the sunlight. "I'll be fine, just didn't get as much sleep as I would have liked. Lots of visitors last night."

Oh boy. "What do you mean?" Of course, I had a pretty good idea.

"Well," Fiona sighed and smoothed out her slacks, "of course there was little Keesha, who had a great deal to talk about, but there were many other dogs who came to me in my dreams—dogs I had known long ago even—seeking guidance on this or that." She frowned and sipped her tea. "It was odd, really. Not only had I never had so many spirits appear in one night, but usually they are varied in form—not just canine."

Her brow furrowed and she looked at me. "Where was it you found Keesha?"

"At the edge of the woods, past the baseball diamond in the park."

I could see the wheels turning as a thought clicked into place. "The old pet cemetery rests in those woods."

Well, that certainly explained a lot. I had forgotten all about that cemetery. I sucked in a breath as I recalled helping Chance bury a pet there once.

Fiona cast me a suspicious look. "You wouldn't happen to know *why* I had an influx of visitors last night, would you, dear?"

I sipped my tea.

Birdie descended the stairs, a trail of lavender following her, and asked, "Would someone explain to me why there is a dog sleeping in my bed?"

"Fiona's was too soft?" I offered.

Birdie gave me her unmissed look.

"Stacy was just about to explain that, Birdie."

Betrayer! I shot Fiona a glare. She usually protected me from Birdie's wrath.

Fiona patted my hand and grinned.

"Okay, but then you need to tell me all about Keesha."

Fiona nodded and Birdie crossed her bare arms, her bracelets clanking together.

I explained how I couldn't find Thor and I was worried so I performed a spell. I took them through it, step-by-step.

Birdie rolled her eyes and leaned against the island when I was finished. She crossed one sandaled foot and her purple skirt fluttered. "So not only had you been drinking, but you performed a spell on your own familiar?"

"Yes." I looked from one to the other. "Is that bad?"

"Bad?" Birdie asked, incredulous. "Is pouring gasoline on a fire bad?"

"Yes."

"What about using a sledgehammer to pound a nail into drywall? Would that be bad?"

I wasn't a carpenter, but I could glean the correct answer from her tone. "Yes, I think that would be bad."

"How about installing a V-8 engine in a scooter?"

Wait, what? "How do you know about V-8 engines?"

Birdie sighed. "The point is, Anastasia, you never cast a spell on your own familiar. When you do, you are combining forces, giving the spell entirely too much power, and the results—as you now know—are disastrous."

"Okay, got it. No more spell casting on Thor. But no one got hurt and most of the dogs are accounted for. Most found their way home."

Fiona stood and moved to the oven where she checked on Thor's lunch. "That is not the way it works. Most likely, you will need to perform a clean-up spell. I'll check into that. In the meantime, I don't suspect Keesha was a product of your spell, but I can't be certain." She twisted the oven dial to off and pulled the bowl out, testing the temperature with her finger.

"What did you find out?" I pushed away from the table and filled a bowl with water.

Fiona placed the food on a mat near the back door and I set the water next to it. I made sure the door leading up the back stairs was shut tight.

"Go ahead and get Thor and then we'll talk."

I opened up the doors at each end of the hallway and whistled. Thor came rumbling through and headed right for his dish. He dug in with enthusiasm, lifting his head and smacking his lips every so often. He ate Fiona's meals absurdly slow; like a foodie at the opening of a new, hot restaurant, he intended to savor and analyze every morsel.

Birdie, Fiona, and I settled around the apothecary table just as Lolly entered from the dining room wearing a wedding dress and yellowed veil. Her two sisters stiffened.

"How are you, dear?" Fiona asked.

Lolly smiled shyly at her. "Happy as I'll ever be." She had more makeup on than usual, and the manner in which it was applied made me wonder if she was about to audition for a silent film.

She said hello to Birdie, who smiled back, and proceeded to the pie safe where the dried herbs were stashed. She fumbled around in there for a minute or so, removing jars and shelves until she emerged with a bouquet of crinkled white roses fastened with a brittle gold ribbon.

Lolly held the flowers in her hand briefly, then bent to sniff them, murmuring to the buds. As she did, the petals perked up and the ribbon that held them together gained some luster.

In fact, so did Lolly.

She smiled first at Birdie, then Fiona, before she looked at me. That's when her smile faltered and a cloud passed over her face.

Fiona jumped up in front of me and said, "Lolly, since I did your makeup, why doesn't Birdie help fix your hair?"

Lolly nodded and gushed, "That would be lovely! My two sisters standing at my side on this most precious day." She hummed a melody unfamiliar to me as she drifted up the back stairwell, Birdie close behind.

What. The. Hell. Lolly's cheese had slid off her pizza long before I could remember, but this was more than just a loose bolt. This was downright creepy.

Fiona got up to refill her iced tea and said, "Now, where were we?"

"No, no." I shook my forefinger. "First, what was that?"

"What?"

"Lolly. What's wrong with her? That isn't the usual mind slippage."

"It's June nineteenth, dear. It's Lolly's wedding day."

My jaw dropped. "She's getting married?"

Fiona chuckled. "No, of course not. This was the day she was to be wed to her sweet Jack forty-nine years ago."

I racked my brain, but for the life of me I could not remember learning that Lolly had ever been engaged.

Fiona tilted her head. "You know, I don't suppose we ever told you about him."

I shook my head. "I don't suppose you did."

Fiona launched into the story as I let Thor outside.

Apparently Jack Moriarty had been quite the catch. "He had piercing blue eyes and sunny hair. He was lean and tall and very funny. He had us all in stitches all the time. Mother and Daddy adored him," Fiona said.

"He grew up here? In Amethyst?"

Fiona nodded. "Lolly and Jack were like two peas in a pod right from the start. They played together, helped each other with their homework, stood up for each other on the playground, that sort of thing. As they got older, their fondness blossomed into love. They could finish each other's sentences, read each other's thoughts. It was amazing how connected they were."

Fiona sighed and peered out the window as if the secrets of the past were just beyond the pane.

I waited for her to continue.

"Jack asked Lolly to marry him when he graduated high school, but Mother wanted them to wait. She had plans for us all to continue our...studies." She stumbled over that last word. "So after a few years, Jack had gone into his father's brewery business and he was doing quite well for himself. Lolly was all grown up and our parents gave them their blessing." Fiona took a long pull of her cold tea. "The wedding was to be right here, in the back garden, and nearly the entire town was invited. I had never seen my big sister so happy."

Fiona paused.

"What happened?" I asked, gently.

She looked at me. "He never arrived."

I sucked in my breath. "Oh. How awful. Poor Lolly."

Fiona rose and took her glass to the sink. The ice rattled around the drain as she dumped it out. "To this day, we don't know what happened to him." She turned toward me. "And we tried *everything*."

I nodded, knowing she meant magic. How awful it must be to find someone you connect with so deeply only to lose him without a trace. How horrible it must be just not *knowing* his fate.

I knew that feeling. I lived that feeling for half of my life when my mother disappeared.

How odd, I thought, to have this raw, open wound in common with Lolly.

Except I knew now what had happened with my mother and where she was. Lolly didn't have that luxury.

I asked, "So the dress, the bouquet?"

Fiona nodded. "We prepare for the occasion every year, just us three, in private."

"And Lolly?"

My great-aunt thought for a moment. "Your aunt Lolly has always been a bit scatterbrained. Mother used to say she was 'away with the fairies.' When Jack never showed up, Lolly did not believe it was by choice but rather some other…force that kept him away." She twirled a lock of hair that had sprung free from a bobby pin. She looked at me as she explained, "She waited for him. Hours turned into days, days grew into weeks, and before we knew it a year had passed. And, well," Fiona sighed, "she simply wasn't ever quite the same."

"Her heart was broken," I said hoarsely.

Fiona smiled. "No, my dear. That's just it. Her heart refused to break. So her mind bore the burden of the wound."

I was still processing that when Lolly and Birdie came down the stairs. Fiona rose to block me from the bride's view.

"Almost ready," Birdie said. Fiona nodded and said, "Be right there."

I watched the eldest Geraghty Girl float out the back door in a worn wedding gown, her youngest sister escorting her train and I thought it was the saddest thing I had ever witnessed.

"Stacy, dear, I need to go, but you can take this with you." She opened up the kitchen catchall drawer and pulled out a notebook. "I wrote down everything from my session with Keesha. Hopefully it's enough to help you find the poor girl's family. She's quite distressed."

She pulled out two small bouquets of lavender from the refrigerator and fluffed the herbs. "You call me if you have any questions, all right, dear?" She kissed me and hustled out the back door, allowing it to bang shut.

I watched through the screen as Fiona handed the second bouquet to Birdie before filing in line behind her.

The picture was surreal. The three of them stood there waiting for a wedding that was supposed to take place nearly half a century ago—a wedding they prepared for every year despite knowing it would not happen. It made my heart ache for Aunt Lolly.

I vowed in that moment that no matter what, I would find out what happened to Jack.

For the briefest moment, Birdie met my eyes.

Chapter 11

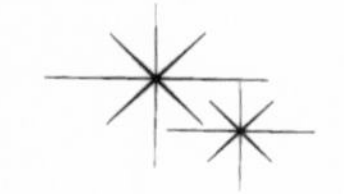

"Dogs are better than human beings because they know but do not tell."

—Emily Dickinson

The parlor was empty as I made my way to the entrance door. Outside, Thor was rolling around on the front lawn, kicking his legs in the air and barking at nothing.

Ah, to be a dog.

"Come on, Thor."

We hopped back in the car and I swung around to my driveway and parked there. I gathered the notebook, the dog, and my bag and we headed inside. Thor immediately curled up on the sofa and I turned the portable air-conditioner on high, grabbed a pair of white shorts and a red tank top, and hit the shower.

It was after one when I finished getting dressed. I twisted my damp hair into a clip, grabbed my amethyst necklace, and tossed the dirty lake towels, my suit, and cover-up in the wash. I was still full from breakfast and Thor was satiated for the time being so I slathered on some sunscreen, slipped into flip-flops, grabbed Fiona's notebook, and headed outside.

Partial shade covered the wicker settee on the porch. Only my legs, which were propped on the railing, were exposed to the sunlight as I opened the cover.

Fiona's normal handwriting was a work of art, the letters beautifully curved and so eloquently designed it looked like a computer font designed specifically for wedding invitations.

A chicken on meth could have scratched out her "session" script. It was hastily scribbled with no paragraphs, no punctuation, and no spaces. Just words incoherently lumped together.

I was able to decipher these on the first page:

Keesha
Pretty
Girl
Smart
Help
Teach
Show

I thought for a minute. Show. Teach. Was she an acting dog? I didn't own a television so I wasn't up on the latest programs. Perhaps for a children's show where she would teach the kids…what?

Or was she perhaps a show dog? An agility performance dog? I wasn't aware of any competitive dog shows in the area, but I made a note to look into that possibility.

On the next page, I found:

Fun
Car
Lady

There was a lady she had known. Her owner? A vet? Trainer? Groomer?

The third page said only:

Bad
Man
Sad

The final page was a jumble of words branching out around one:

Thor

It wasn't his name so much that disturbed me as the words around it: *Good, Boy, Nice, Like, Play, Friend, Brave.*

Uh-oh.

I shut the notebook and leaned my head back. I didn't realize Fiona's ability was stilted. I thought I would be reading this dog's whole life story, not just random thoughts. But maybe Fiona knew the whole story and she just scribbled these notes down. I walked around to the side of the cottage where I could see the back garden.

They were still in formation. Waiting for a phantom groom.

Through the open window, Thor yawned loudly as he jumped off the couch. He nudged the door open with his snout, lumbered onto the porch, and stretched deeply.

I sat back on the settee and he greeted me by sniffing the back of my neck like it was a turkey leg. Truth be told, it was a bit refreshing in this heat.

I twisted to face him and said, "Please do not encourage Keesha. She seems to have a crush on you."

The reasonable side of me was well aware that responsible pet owners spayed and neutered their animals, but Thor, as my familiar, was different. And since he'd come to me with all his parts fully functional, I thought it best not to alter the original design.

Besides, what if all his magic was stored in the luggage compartment?

We were nose to nose and he gave me his most meaningful look and sneezed in my face, covering me with dirt and sand.

I popped up. "Agh! That's disgusting."

I dashed inside to rinse off the mucus and put the notebook on my desk. When I came back outside, Thor's tail was thumping against the porch boards and Leo was walking up the driveway. He was wearing the same faded jeans he had on earlier, accompanied by a white polo shirt with an Amethyst PD logo in the corner. Standard cop shades hid his eyes.

"Hey, Chief," I said.

As soon as my voice hit the wind, I heard the high-pitched yap of my nemesis.

"Geez, you brought Cujo?"

Thor's ears perked up at the noise and he sidled over to me, leaned against my hip. He cocked his head, trying to decipher where the sound was coming from.

Leo said, "He's in the car with the air-conditioner running, so don't worry. Thought it best not to take a chance with your bodyguard on duty."

"Not to mention it could get confusing with them sharing a name. I mean, how would we tell them apart?"

"I changed his name, smart-ass."

"To what? Odin? Zeus? Hercules?"

"Scrappy."

I made a face.

"What? It was your suggestion. Besides, he is scrappy."

I held up my hands. "Hey, it's none of my business. I can't believe you didn't find his family, though. Someone must be wondering where he is. He looked well taken care of."

"Gus has been working on it, but so far no luck."

"So what brings you by?"

Leo held up a plastic bag with a tooth-marked cell phone sealed inside.

I asked, "Do you know who he is—I mean was?"

"Not yet, but I do know he hasn't been down there that long. I also know who he was looking for."

I perched forward. "Who?" If I could get an answer, perhaps I could return the watch to whoever it was meant for and put his soul to rest.

"You."

I could feel the blood drain from my face as my body went cold. Friday's phone call replayed in my mind.

"Stacy Justice?"

"Speaking."

"Stacy Justice the second, right?"

"Yes."

"I just thought you should know that I have the tapes."

"What tapes?" I asked.

The man on the phone swore softly. "You haven't gone through his files yet, have you?"

"Whose files? What you are talking about?"

"It wasn't an accident," the man said.

"Who is this?"

"Your father was murdered."

Leo's voice burst through my thoughts. "Stacy. Stace? Are you okay?"

I wanted to pass out, collapse into a chair, scream—anything but stand here and pretend as if my world had not just spun out of control. But I couldn't. Leo couldn't know until I knew the whole truth.

I took a deep breath, told myself to get a grip, that it still might have been a prank. Leo was watching, waiting for a response, and I had to give him one.

"Sorry. It's just the heat. Let's go inside."

Leo followed me to the kitchen and I grabbed us each a bottled water. Thor came in too and heaved himself in front of the air-conditioner.

"So, he tried to call me?" I asked after taking a huge gulp.

"Not your private line, your work line. It's a burner phone, can't be traced. Your work number was the only number he dialed. Did you get any phone calls on Friday that were out of the ordinary?"

"Nope," I lied, averting my eyes.

Leo studied me for a moment. "Are you sure? Nothing that might seem even remotely related to the body we fished out of the lake? Around noon?"

I gave my best performance of trying to search my mind for information.

"Nothing rings a bell."

"Interesting." He uncapped his water and sipped it slowly. "The body that you reported, the one that"—he used air quotes here—"Thor drudged up, nothing connects you to it at all?"

"What's with the air quotes? You don't believe me?" I narrowed my eyes at him.

"Cut the bull, Stacy. The guy had a cement block attached to his ankle and that lake is about forty feet deep. There was no boat floating on the water, which means he didn't tie it to his own foot."

No boat. Of course it wasn't suicide. "A cement block? Is that on the record? Can I print that?"

Leo sighed, drank the rest of his water, and grabbed his sunglasses. I could feel frustration rolling off him in waves as he approached the door, but there was no way I could tell him how I had actually discovered the body. *You see, Leo, it was like this. The dude dragged me down into the depths of the lake à la* Friday the Thirteenth Part One*, and now I'm bound by a soggy oath to put his soul to rest.*

Yeah, that would not go over well.

And perhaps telling him about the phone call would have been the right move, but there was something I had to do first.

Leo paused at the door and said, "Please call me if you remember anything. Even if you suspect something or get a feeling about something or…whatever, please just let me know." He turned back to me. "The information this guy was going to relay to you may have gotten him killed. If that's the case, then you might be in someone's crosshairs. Be careful."

Then he left.

I stared through the screen, watching him walk down the pathway toward his vehicle.

He was right, I knew. And as soon as I took care of one thing, I would tell him everything. The phone call, the watch, Dad—everything.

Leo's car motored away, the white tiger sprawled across the roof.

Yep, he would hear all about it since I might need his help anyway.

And someone else might need it too.

Because if I found out my father was murdered, Heaven wouldn't be able to save the son of a bitch responsible.

Chapter 12

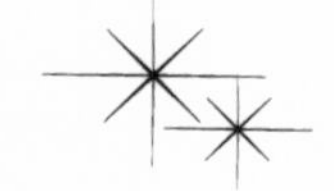

"I was a dog in a past life. Really. I'll be walking down the street and dogs will do a sort of double take. Like, Hey, I know him."

—William H. Macy

So much for my relaxing weekend. I had a collie who needed to find her way home, a dead guy who needed peace, a musician who may or may not know something about said dead guy, a groom missing for half a century, and oh yeah—the little matter of lost tapes and my father's possible homicide.

Lazy days of summer these were not.

I changed into jeans and sneakers and tucked my hair into a Cubs hat. Next I called Cinnamon, hoping she could accompany me on what I was about to do.

Tony answered the phone. "That game really wore her out and she's expecting a big crowd tonight so she's catching a nap before work. You want me to leave her a message?"

"No, that's fine. I'll catch up with her later."

I was about to hang up when I decided Tony might be able to save me some legwork. "Hey, Tony, is your auto body shop the only one that tows in this area?"

"For seventy years. Why?"

"Just following a lead. And all the cars that are abandoned go to the Junkyard Graveyard off White Hope Road, right?"

"That's right."

"Okay. Thanks."

I texted Derek. *Road trip?*

He texted back. *Heard about the body on my scanner. Pick me up?*

Wear grubby.

Always do when I'm with you.

Thor was snoring like a hibernating bear. I decided to let him sleep. I went into the bedroom and grabbed my workbag from the closet. I always kept a pad of paper, pens, and a recorder in there and I figured I might need 'em on this trip.

My eyes traipsed over the Blessed Book and I hesitated.

Could there be some prediction in there about Lolly's Jack? Surely Birdie and Fiona would have scoured it from cover to cover by now, but was there something they missed? A message of warning that he was in danger, perhaps? Or a clue that hinted he wasn't the man for Lolly?

I set the bag aside and scooted across the carpet, reaching for the book. When I touched it, an electric shock jolted my finger.

"Ouch." I shook my hand out and left the book where it was.

There was no time for looking into that right now, I decided. Lolly had waited forty-nine years; surely she could wait a little while longer.

I closed the closet door, hoisted the bag over my shoulder, grabbed my keys, and walked outside.

The newscaster on the car radio said it would be a high of eighty-two degrees today, but it felt more like a hundred and two when I pulled up to Derek's apartment.

He hopped inside and said, "Damn, it's cooking out there." He pointed the passenger vent at his face, soaking up the cool air.

"Where's your camera?"

He grinned and reached inside his shirt pocket. He pulled out a pair of sunglasses and put them on, looking straight ahead.

"Thanks for the fashion show, Derek, but I need your camera. The camera on my phone sucks."

He turned his head to face me, his movements robotic, and tapped a finger to the edge of his sunglasses. He pulled them down, slowly, and flashed his brown eyes at me, wiggling his eyebrows.

"You're beginning to annoy me," I said.

"I just took your picture."

"What do you mean, you just took my picture?"

He tipped his head so that his right eye was angled at my ear. "Now I'm recording your cleavage."

I smacked his shoulder.

"Yo, easy, woman!"

"Quit messing around, will you?"

"I'm not." Derek removed his sunglasses and said, "The latest addition to my collection." He tilted them toward me as he spoke, pointing to the right arm of the sunglasses. "This is the video/audio camera and this"—he shifted the shades and pointed to the left arm—"is the still camera."

He slipped the sunglasses back on and grinned at me. "Admit it, you think it's badass."

I have to say, I was impressed. "Totally badass, dude."

He faced forward again, crossed his arms over his Abercrombie & Fitch T-shirt, and said, "Fo' shizzle."

I paused, put the car in reverse, and said, "This better be a phase, Snoop Dogg."

The Junkyard Graveyard, about ten miles outside of town, was where automobiles, motorcycles, boats, RVs, and even large appliances went to die. It was one of those places that takes on a life of its own in a small community. That is to say, it became an urban legend of sorts so teenagers often dared each other to hike through the grounds at midnight, or camp out in the adjacent woods, or—the greatest challenge of all—knock on the trailer of its owner, Mr. Scoog.

I had never succumbed to the legend myself. Growing up in the Geraghty house was kind of a living myth in its own right, but the rumors were that Mr. Scoog was a beastly man with a hook for a hand, a glass eye he liked to hurl at people, and a pet falcon that would rip your ears off if you got too close to the property.

I believed all that as much as I believed in the Easter bunny.

It felt like I had driven too far, but then I saw the sign for the street leading to the Graveyard.

"Finally," I said, slowing the car.

Derek leaned forward and took his sunglasses off. "You're messing with me, right?"

I glanced at him quickly, not daring to take my eyes off this unfamiliar road for too long. "What do you mean?"

"Devil's Ladder Road? Where the hell are we going?" He squirmed a little in his seat. "No pun intended."

"We're checking out an accident vehicle."

"Why? I thought the stiff was a floater. I didn't hear anything about a car accident."

"Give me a minute." I leaned closer to the windshield, looking for some indication that I was where I needed to be.

We passed a sign that read: NO TRESPASSERS! Just after that, the paved road broke up, and we found ourselves meandering along a rocky dirt path flanked by overgrown weeds and low-hanging tree branches that scraped the car. It was an eerie sound. Like an unidentifiable animal sharpening its claws for a kill. The tree canopy grew thicker the farther along the path we moved until it eventually blocked the sun. I slowed the car down to a near crawl. There were no signs yet that we were heading in the right direction and I thought that perhaps my memory had failed me. I had never come here myself, but I could have sworn this was the way. The name of the road had been etched in my mind since I'd heard the adults whisper it around me in the aftermath of the crash that killed my father.

A crow swooped in front of the windshield, screeching and flapping its wings as if reprimanding us. It glided over to a smashed-in school bus and parked on the exposed engine, glaring at us. I sucked in my breath.

Derek let out a low whistle, turning his head for a last look at the yellow-and-black wreckage as we rolled by. "Did you see that? Looked like it was cut in half."

"It was," I told him.

"No way."

I nodded. "Happened in the seventies. A train."

He didn't ask any more questions and I didn't offer any answers.

Some stories were better left untold.

We saw a KEEP OUT! sign on the left, an old Roper stove and a tire-less Chevy pickup on the right, and just beyond that, another creature cackled.

And something thumped the hood.

I wondered briefly if it was the white tiger, but I had a feeling this was more of a flesh-and-blood animal than a spirit guide.

"Why do I have the urge to piss my pants?" Derek asked just as the scratches sounded on the roof. "Seriously, Justice, what is the freaking plan here?" He was white-knuckling the dashboard, trying to see around the visor. "Because I'm starting to get the feeling like I'm about to become the first victim of a serial killer who's been writing his manifesto for years."

"Don't be so dramatic. Besides, why you? He could kill me first."

"Bitch, please. You know the young, good-looking black dude always gets it first."

I rolled my eyes. More wrecks appeared as we traveled down the road. We were getting close.

Then an enormous bird landed on the passenger-side windshield wiper, and Derek screamed like a little girl in a spook house.

He scrambled to lock his door and I stopped the car. "What is that—a pterodactyl? Jesus, lord!"

The aluminum motor home was about ten feet away from us looking like a traveling beer can. I couldn't help but feel a little nervous at the bullet holes in the side, but the plastic begonias out front seemed to give the impression that Mr. Scoog had at least tried to soften up the place.

Derek saw the sign before I did. THE JUNKYARD GRAVEYARD. He looked at me, face deadpan. "I am not getting out of this car. You're on your own."

"Don't be ridiculous." I unlatched my seat belt. "You can't possibly believe those stories."

He crinkled his brow. "What stories?"

Oops. "Nothing."

"What stories?" he repeated.

The bird pecked the windshield once and cocked its beak at Derek.

Derek shook his head, eyeing the bird. "Nuh-uh. No. Way. I am not getting out of this car. If you want to deliver yourself to some flesh-eating dragon, have at it. I can only imagine what the dude who lives in the Silver Bullet Mobile looks like."

The dude who lived in the Silver Bullet Mobile stepped out the narrow doorway. If "beastly" could ever have accurately described him then it was a safe bet he had been locked in a dryer for twenty years.

He was wearing a grammatically incorrect "Bro's Before Ho's" T-shirt and jeans that were a challenge for his belt to hold on to. He looked about a hundred and fifty years old, and while there was a can of Old Style in his hand, it was held in place by four fingers and a thumb—not a hook.

I looked at Derek. "Happy? You going to tell me you're afraid of a guy who's older than Santa Claus and about as heavy as his sack on December twenty-sixth?"

"You going to tell me why we're here?"

"I got a lead, okay? It may link to the body they pulled from the lake."

The man waved enthusiastically from his porch.

"Fine," Derek said.

He followed me out through the driver's-side door since the bird was still perched near the passenger's side.

The ground was dusty. Dry. As if it never rained in this part of town, despite all the vibrantly green foliage.

I pasted a smile on my face and waved to Mr. Scoog. Derek walked ever so slowly, the bird trailing him on foot, making little cawing sounds with each step.

We finally made it to the foot of the porch.

"Hello. Are you Mr. Scoog?" I asked.

Derek tried to shoo the bird away with his foot and I elbowed him.

"I sure am! And who might you be, good-lookin'?" He flashed his gums at me.

I reached in my bag for a card, slapping away a mosquito. "My name is Stacy Justice. I write for the *Amethyst Globe*." Mr. Scoog reached across the railing for my business card with his free hand and set the beer down on a rickety metal table.

"Boy, I gotta tell you, little lady, my eyesight just ain't what it used to be. 'Scuse me a second."

I waited for Mr. Scoog to step inside to retrieve his glasses. He surprised me by yanking his eye right out of its socket.

Guess the rumor about the glass eye was true.

Derek yelped and the bird glided up to the porch railing.

Mr. Scoog slapped his knee, then pointed at Derek and me. "Gotcha!"

"Oh," I said stupidly. "You sure did there, you…rascal."

Derek gave me an eat-shit look and I mouthed *sorry* to him.

The bird was still studying my coworker.

"Hey there, young fella, no hard feelings." Mr. Scoog extended his hand to Derek, still chuckling.

"Not at all." Derek's voice was strained until Mr. Scoog's hand slipped off midshake. Then he yelled, "Agh!" clutching the prosthetic appendage.

Mr. Scoog's face turned bright red, his mouth wide open.

Nothing came out.

"Is he laughing?" I asked out of the corner of my mouth.

"How should I know?" Derek slapped a mosquito that could have landed at O'Hare.

The bird cocked his head toward Mr. Scoog. Suddenly a happy bellow exploded from the tiny man.

"Did you see the look on his face, Liberty?" Mr. Scoog asked the bird, nodding. The bird moved her body up and down. To us he said, "We don't entertain much."

Derek took a step away from the porch, eyes glued to the bird.

"Well, she won't hurt you. Don't worry about Liberty." Mr. Scoog slipped a sleeve over his nub and Liberty climbed on his arm. "Yep, she only eats rodents and small animals. Squirrels, rabbits, fox, that sort of thing.

Helps out a great deal scarin' pests away." Mr. Scoog tilted his beer can toward Liberty and she ripped it from his hands, shotgunned the thing like a frat boy, and tossed it over her head.

I wondered if Liberty could eat a Chihuahua.

"Kids, what brings ya by?"

I fished through my bag until I found the old newspaper clipping of my father's accident. I'd attached an intact photo of the car to the article. "Do you recall this vehicle? It came through here about fourteen years ago."

Mr. Scoog looked at the photo first, then the news piece. He scanned it, frowned, and said, "Sorry, can't say as I do." He handed the article back to me. "Memory ain't what it used to be either."

I looked around the property. There were acres and acres of crumpled vehicles as far as I could see. Some were intertwined with tree branches, most rusted out beyond repair; many were now home to stray animals.

All of them told a story. Now, I was interested in only one.

"I don't suppose we could take a look around?" I said in the sweetest voice I could muster.

Derek looked at me as if I had lost my marbles.

Mr. Scoog wrinkled his nose. "Sorry, girlie, it's too dangerous to just go traipsin' through them wrecks without knowin' where your aim is. Can't have you kids gettin' hurt."

I thanked him for his time and we turned to go.

Damn! I really wanted to get a look at the car. Maybe there was something the police missed? Hell, maybe the files the caller mentioned were in the car.

"But you know..." Mr. Scoog said.

Derek was already opening the car door. He cracked a window to release some steam.

I turned. "Yes?"

"This was a local wreck, right? I keep good records, and any local vehicles and whatnot I usually don't scrap, outta respect an' all."

"So could you take me to it?"

Mr. Scoog shook his head. "Not me. That long ago, the car'd be way out on back lot number three and I don't get 'round so good anymore." He reached into a vintage 7-Up cooler, grabbed another beer, and swigged. "But Liberty here knows the way." He lifted his arm and said, "She seems to have taken a liking to your friend there. She'd be glad to help."

I grinned wide and slowly turned to give Derek, who was already belted in, two thumbs up.

He flipped me the bird.

Chapter 13

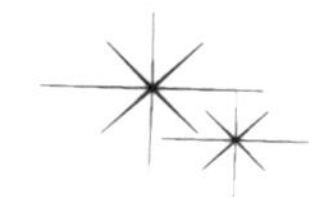

"You owe me big time for this one, Justice," Derek said.

He was seething and I can't say that I blamed him. Liberty, we discovered, was a golden eagle, one of the largest birds of prey in North America. Apparently Scoog had been into falconry for years and was well known in those circles. A sanctuary had found Liberty a few years before, lethargic and losing weight after the death of her life mate. Her depression was severe enough that they feared she was slowly committing suicide so they called Scoog. He nursed her back to health and now she looked upon him as a sort of father figure, resigned to being single forever.

Until today.

"This thing weighs a ton." Derek wore a long glove that resembled a leather oven mitt, and Liberty cheerfully rode shotgun on his arm, cooing and occasionally rubbing Derek's cheek with her feathered head.

It was quite a sight.

Scoog had drawn out a rough map, so we had a general idea of where my father's car came to rest, but the terrain was too rugged to drive. We had to hoof it.

"I think it's just past that willow tree," I said.

I wasn't sure what the purpose of the bird guide was until we were nearly swallowed by a sinkhole. From what I could gather by the way the eagle squawked and swooped down as we approached it, her main purpose was to divert us away from dangerous areas.

A little over twenty minutes later, we found lot number three and the car. My stomach did a somersault as soon as I laid eyes on my father's death trap.

I must have looked shaken because Derek asked me, "You okay? You need some water? This heat is obnoxious."

I ignored him and approached the blue sedan. I didn't dare touch it—not yet. I needed to center and calm myself first. I could feel my eyes getting wet and a shiver tore through my body.

Memories flooded back and I was so overwhelmed, I had to sit for fear that I would faint.

Dad taking me to the movies. Mom making tacos for dinner. Dad giving me a tour of his office—the very office I worked in today—while Mom supplied homemade beauty products to an organic shop on Main Street. We lived in our own little house on a quiet dead-end street. We had a porch swing, a flower garden, and a one-car garage.

It was perfect.

And then…it wasn't.

Finally Derek said, "This was your dad's car, wasn't it, Stacy?"

I have never been an emotional person. In my line of work, especially reporting on crime in the city of Chicago, you learn to train yourself to keep emotions in check.

Rarely did I cry, and when I did, it certainly wasn't in front of anyone. I kept my back to Derek as I nodded and quickly wiped my eyes dry.

"Okay, I know you didn't drag me out here just to look at it. What's going on?"

I told him about the phone call, the body from the lake, and my suspicions. Told him about everything except the watch I had retrieved from the water.

"I just had to come here and check it out for myself, you know? I can read the accident reports and Leo may let me view the photos, but…um…"

Geez, how else could I explain it? I couldn't say, *I'm a witch and the Seeker of Justice, so you know, maybe the answer will magically appear*?

Thankfully, I didn't have to.

"Hey, I get it. And if the accident connects to the guy from the lake, Parker might just give us both a raise." He lifted his arm as Mr. Scoog taught him and released Liberty. She flew to a nearby tire stack.

Parker. Maybe he would know what the caller meant about the tapes. Heck, I had no idea what Dad was even working on when he died. There was never any reason to look into it, because there was never any doubt that his death was an accident. First thing tomorrow morning, I had to go through my father's files.

Derek began snapping pictures while I made my way around the smashed car. I didn't touch it yet; I was still absorbing the shape it was in from a small distance. It looked like it had been through a trash compactor, all jagged glass and crushed metal. No one could have survived a crash like this car had been through. As far as I knew, his was the only car the truck had hit. Which meant the brown splotches must have been his blood.

The realization of that caused me to double over into a fit of dry heaves. I kept repeating in my head what my mother had told me. *He didn't suffer, Stacy. They said his life left in an instant.*

Dear Gods, please let that be true.

I took another deep breath to steady my heartbeat. I couldn't get in the driver's seat, which was where I thought I might have been able to conjure a vision, because it was gone.

I decided to crawl underneath the frame. Maybe the brake lines had been cut? The fuel line? There were any number of ways to tamper with a vehicle to cause a crash, but coupled with icy conditions and an eighteen-wheeler spinning out of control, who would have checked for foul play?

I thought about the driver of the truck. I never even asked about him in the midst of my self-centered teenage grief. Had he survived? And if so, would he remember anything?

Nothing seemed out of the ordinary to me under the car that didn't match the rest of the wreckage. No wires cut that I could tell, but then again, I wasn't a mechanic. Cin or Tony might be able to verify that for sure.

I crawled back out and asked Derek to snap some shots of the undercarriage. I pulled my notebook from my bag and jotted down a to-do list.

Review accident report. Research truck driver, trucking company. What was he hauling? Dig up Dad's old files. Ask Parker about tapes—

Something whizzed by my ear and I heard a loud clink.

"What was that?" Derek asked from under the car. He couldn't see much thanks to the sunglasses camera.

Another clank, and then another exploded into the rear fender.

I dropped to the ground and crawled under the car with Derek, army style.

"What are you doing?"

"Someone's shooting at us!" I looked around frantically from the space beneath the car. Saw no feet, no legs. Didn't know where the shots were coming from. He or she could have been hiding in a tree, up on a hill, or behind the Magic Mystery Machine, which we also passed on our trek out here.

We were in a wide-open field, armed only with a pair of sunglasses and Big Bird.

Chapter 14

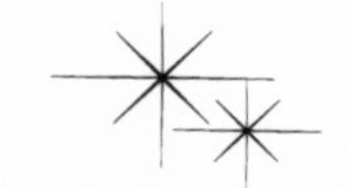

After two more dings, Derek said, "Dang, woman! Why are people always trying to kill you?"

"I don't know. I'm a very likeable person."

I crawled toward the back tire and peeked out into the landscape.

Lots of open space.

"What's the plan?" Derek asked.

"I didn't have a contingency plan for being shot at."

"You should always have a plan for that. You're like a psycho magnet. I'd be packing twenty-four seven if I had your track record."

"I'll put it on my to-do list, right after *don't get killed*."

The hubcap took a hit as Derek reached for his phone. "Shit, I left my phone in your car."

"Mine's in my bag."

Derek fished my phone out from the bag slung across my back.

"No signal."

The stack of tires Liberty had perched on was to my left. An antique washing machine sat a few yards from that.

But where was the shooter?

"Derek, do you see anything on your side? Anything to take cover in?"

If it had been a pro—a sharpshooter—we most likely would have been dead already.

"I got a giant Big Boy head, a Coca-Cola sign, and a refrigerator door. There's a tractor about fifty feet from that."

I scooted over to see what he was looking at. The shots all seemed to come toward the front of the car. The far side would be our best chance. The refrigerator door was an old Westinghouse, not so different from what was in Birdie's kitchen. Those things were built like tanks.

Another bullet hit the dirt near my hand.

"Count of three, run for that fridge door. We'll use it like a shield. Ready?"

Derek nodded. Then he said, "Wait, is it one, two, three then go? Or one, two, then go?"

"One, two, then go."

I grabbed the back tire with both hands for a second, hoping for a sign, a vision, anything that would penetrate my mind with the truth. I shut my eyes. *Please, Daddy, talk to me!*

Not my father, nor his killer, but I did get something.

The white tiger flashed in my mind and unleashed a deafening roar. I saw teeth dripping with saliva, muscles bulging from her throat like a road map, and in that split second, I knew two things.

One (and most urgent), we had to get the hell out of there. Fast.

The other (and most astonishing) was that my mother was somehow sending me her spirit guide.

Chapter 15

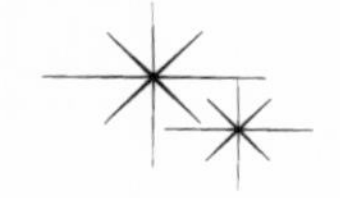

"One. Two. Three!"

We scrambled out from under the vehicle and ran in a crouch all the way to the refrigerator door. Derek lifted it by the handle and I ducked behind it just in time.

A shot connected with the metal.

Running with a hundred-pound refrigerator door as a shield is not as easy as it sounds. I would have really loved a pair of Wonder Woman bracelets right then.

"Geez, this thing weighs more than that damn bird!" Derek said.

Liberty! Where the heck was she?

Derek was usually faster than I was, but he was running backward, holding the bulk of the door. I faced front, looking for anything to take cover in. There was the tractor, a snowmobile to the left of that, and one lone oak tree beyond.

I made an executive decision. "Derek, the tractor isn't too far, just hang on to that door."

A shot splintered part of the tree and I veered us away from it. The tractor was a gigantic John Deere yellow and green number, which meant it was big enough to hide behind for the time it would take to check my phone for a signal.

Two more shots sailed into our makeshift shield.

"Are we there yet?" Derek asked, and then he screamed. "Shit! OW! Shit!"

"Oh my God, Derek? Are you shot?"

"Son of a—geez that hurt!"

"Almost there. Hang on!"

The tractor was two steps away. More shots zinged off an empty gas can.

Just as we circled around the machine, Derek screamed again and I heard a crunch.

"Are you hit again? What happened?"

"I wasn't hit at all. I think I stepped on a nail back there, but that sack of monkey dung just shot my shades off my face!"

Oh no. I looked down. "And I just stepped on them. Damn, we needed those pictures!" I was pretty sure any evidence left on that car would be gone if we ever got out of here alive.

"Forget the pictures! You owe me two hundred fifty bucks, man."

At that moment, Liberty swooped down, screaming. She soared back up, took a longing look at Derek, and flapped majestically toward the path we had just taken.

"I think she's trying to buy us some time. Come on!" I said.

Derek scooped up what was left of his spy shades and shoved them into his shirt pocket. I checked my phone again. Still no signal, which didn't really surprise me.

We were in the middle of nowhere.

I quickly scanned the junkyard. The snowmobile, I noticed, had a smashed front end. In fact, most of the cars around were badly injured in one capacity or another. The tractor, however, seemed in tip-top shape.

"Derek, maybe we can climb in the cab."

"And then what? That's probably not bulletproof glass, Lucy," he said in a Hispanic accent.

Right.

"Maybe there's a weapon inside. Farmers carry shotguns, right? Give me a boost."

I slipped my foot into his clasped hands and he hoisted me onto the bulging tire. I squealed like a little girl. "Derek, keys! There are keys in the ignition with an eagle key ring. This must be Scoog's."

"Great. You know how to drive one of these things?"

"How hard can it be?"

"You realize it's an all-glass cab, a one-seater, and probably goes about ten miles an hour, right?"

"If you have a better idea, Negative Nancy, I'm all ears."

He didn't.

The nail in Derek's foot banished any argument about who would drive, so I climbed in and he followed. Then I fired the beast up.

Or tried to.

The engine didn't turn over.

Tried again. Nothing.

"Stop that! You need to put your foot on the clutch or you'll flood the engine," Derek said. "You do know how to drive stick, right?"

"Cinnamon taught me awhile ago. I think I remember."

Shoot. I didn't realize it was a manual transmission. There was a long lever that looked like a parking brake. I released that and Derek nearly sailed through the windshield.

"Sorry."

He glared at me.

"I'll get it." It wasn't like I spent my weekends tilling the fields or attending tractor pulls, although considering how most of my weekends turned out, I may give it a try next time.

A bullet hit something in the back of the machine just as I pushed in the clutch. I stepped on the gas and the tractor jerked forward, then lunged back a few times before I finally found the balance. When I turned the key one last time, the engine rumbled to life.

I bobbed and weaved as I shifted the four-wheeled monstrosity into its highest gear. I figured it was harder to hit a moving target. Derek was scrunched against the door like one of those suction-cup car ornaments.

"Keep an eye on that phone and call Leo as soon as you get a signal."

"Gee, and I was just going to ride it out and see what happens," Derek said sarcastically. "I'm in pain here! I plan to call the po-po, the fire department, an ambulance, and the National Guard! Then I'm calling the closest nuthouse to have you evaluated."

"Oh please, it's not like you got shot," I said, glancing at his foot. It was gushing blood. One nail could do all that damage? Thank the Goddess he didn't have time to examine it. Derek wasn't exactly Rambo. Every time he sees his own blood—and I mean a freaking paper cut—he faints. I didn't want him to notice the horror on my face, so I kept talking as I wiggled my bag off my shoulder and laid it over his feet.

"Besides, you're the one with the feathered girlfriend. Speaking of which, do you see her?" I chewed my lip, trying desperately to maneuver the tractor away from stray cars, antique lawn mowers, and small rodents. "Hope she doesn't get hurt."

Derek moved his head slightly. "I can hear her. But I don't hear anything else."

I listened. He was right. The pinging sounds had ceased. At least for the moment.

"Go, Liberty," I said.

It was a bumpy ride for several minutes as we dodged a ghostly motorcycle, a rotting pontoon boat, and, ahead in the distance, some sort of metal sculpture shaped like a dinosaur. That dinosaur looked familiar.

I searched the recesses of my brain until I recalled a field trip I took as a child to what the teacher called Art in the Park. A local metalworks artist and welder who lived just off the highway welcomed classes to tour his property and his many works of art. It was all made from recycled metal such as wheel rims, bed frames, wrenches, farm equipment, saws—even tractor parts. It made sense now. He must have acquired a lot of the material from Scoog. From what I understood, he was popular with tourists from Chicago's North Shore and trendy shop owners from Wicker Park, Logan Square, and Boystown.

We must have been close to his property.

Surely he would have a phone.

"Derek, what's the name of that road?"

He pulled out a small film canister from his back pocket. With one flick, it transformed into an extended single-vision scope, like a ship's captain might use.

"Does everyone shop at the spy store but me?" Aunt Lolly, I'd learned the hard way, loved that place.

"It's filled with some cool stuff, let me tell you." Derek winced in pain as he shifted his weight and angled his body forward. "Looks like Blue Diamond Drive."

"Do you think the GPS will work on the phone without any network coverage?"

"If it can ping off a satellite, then sure."

"Give it a try."

I slowed the tractor down when we reached a dirt road. There were no cars coming as far as I could see and the dinosaur was farther away than I thought. The size had deceived me and I didn't see a house or even a mailbox nearby.

"The GPS is not zeroing in on us, but it's giving a map of the area. Looks like whatever was last plugged into it is lingering."

"Do you see the road anywhere on there?"

"Yep. Looks like we're about fifteen miles from town, and White Hope snakes around the other side of Blue Diamond."

The phone beeped the low-battery cry.

"Turn it off. Can't afford to lose any more juice right now," I said.

I forged ahead, glancing often at Derek. He looked pale. "There should be a water in my bag. Might be some snacks too."

The tractor bounced along the dirt road, the hum of the engine the only sound for miles. It was hotter than Hades' oven inside so I asked Derek to open his window and I did the same. He handed me half the bottle of water and I accepted a sip but gave him the rest. I had no idea how much blood he had lost, but the stench of fear and our own body odor was enough to make anyone pass out at that point. For a moment, I considered tearing directly over to White Hope Road and just driving this behemoth mobile right down the center line, hoping someone would call the cops.

I spotted a domed house, fit for a hobbit, in a thicket of trees. It was flanked by two metal knights.

"Derek, is that an oasis or is that really a house?"

"It's either a house or we've stumbled upon the lost land of Camelot."

I smiled. "Let's hope Merlin's home."

Chapter 16

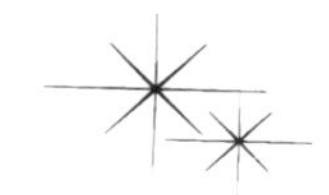

The poor man came out of his home looking like aliens had just landed.

I guess it wasn't every day a tractor pulled into his driveway carrying a local reporter and a photographer who was cursing and bleeding all over the gravel.

I tried to get Derek to wait inside the vehicle, but he refused. Actually, refused is putting it mildly. What he said was, "Are you crazy? Let me guess, you think if I sit here in this heat I'll melt into a chocolate bunny that you can gobble up? Who-wee." He rubbed his stomach. "I'm Stacy and I'd love me a chocolate bunny."

Okay, not only did that make no sense, but I hadn't eaten a chocolate bunny since I was five, and I was pretty sure that statement was racist.

He was seriously losing coherency. I had to make sure he didn't inspect his foot.

"Fine, but just stay here, okay? And"—I glanced over my shoulder for emphasis—"keep an eye on this guy." That might keep him from looking down.

Derek crossed his arms, lifted his chin, and adjusted an invisible hat in an attempt to look all badass gangsta.

When I turned back around the man was just a few feet behind me. "Can I help you with something?"

His eyes sparkled with curiosity. He had a grease-stained rag in his hands and he was polishing a brass pipe, but the rest of his appearance gave the impression of a freshly retired teacher ready to hit the links.

"Pipe!" Derek screamed.

I turned around and gave Derek the OK sign.

He nodded.

"You in some kind of trouble?" the man asked me.

There were about thirty different ways to answer that question and I was ready to start with the very bad man and his endless supply of ammo, but my savior pushed me gently aside and said, "My stars! Son, what happened to your foot?"

Well, hell.

That was all it took. Derek ogled his bloody appendage, shrieked, and collapsed to the ground like a deflated balloon.

I turned to smile at the man whom I hoped would let us in his house.

I quickly ran through a false scenario. We were lost, had been in the heat all day with nothing to eat or drink, then Derek stepped on God knows what, and when we stumbled across a tractor it was do or die.

I left out most of the "die" part. This guy had heard and seen enough.

He rushed to help me carry Derek inside and we laid him on the cool tile in the foyer. I could see what had impaled his foot. A generous portion of a broken beer bottle.

"This is my studio, you see. I don't have too many luxuries. No Internet, no kitchen, but there is a bathroom and a landline. In the far corner of the bathroom"—he pointed down a short hall—"there are some old towels."

I thanked him and ran to wet a towel down. When I came back, he was on the phone and I knelt to tend to Derek.

"Yes, it looks like a puncture wound. I am at fifty-three Blue Diamond Drive. My name is Frank Moriarty."

I dropped the towel.

He hung up after giving the emergency operator a few more details.

"Did you say Frank Moriarty?"

"Yes, that's right."

Moriarty. That was the name of Lolly's Jack.

The phone rang.

Frank answered it and said, "Yes. Yes. She is. Would you like to speak with her?" A pause, a confused look.

I mopped Derek's head with the wet towel.

"All right." He hung up.

I continued taking care of my fallen colleague.

"Um..." Frank said.

"Yes?"

"Well, I assume from the description given to me that you are Stacy Justice?"

"I am."

"Would you mind telling me then, seeing as you're in my studio and all, why the police chief asked me to detain you?"

I had to think fast. Thing was, there was really no good reason why this man should not usher me right out the door but…

"Does the name Lolly Geraghty ring a bell?"

He hesitated, seeming to recall a faraway memory. "My stars, I haven't heard that name in years." He scratched his closely trimmed beard. "She was a friend of my cousin's a long time ago."

"Your cousin?"

Derek began to stir and I fought the urge to kick him.

"Yes. Jack disappeared years ago. Right before he was to marry Lolly. Did you know her?"

The redirection was working. He no longer seemed to care that I may have been a fugitive.

"She's my great-aunt. I'm told they were quite an item."

Frank sat down on a bench. "I'm afraid I don't know much about any of that. You see, Jack disappeared close to fifty years ago and we weren't from town. My parents lived outside of Chicago."

"So what brought you here to Amethyst?"

"My grandparents left me this land when they passed. I always enjoyed the area, so on one visit I bought a little cottage in town and decided to use this land for my workshop."

There was a knock at the door. "Paramedics."

Derek was just coming to, but he saw the green glass protruding from his foot and passed out again.

The paramedics rolled out a gurney and gently lifted Derek onto it. Most of the EMTs in Amethyst were volunteers and I recognized the young woman. "Stacy, did you want to ride with him?"

"Oh, um..." I glanced at Mr. Moriarty. He didn't seem too eager to detain me. I reached inside my bag for my card and handed it to him. Then I pulled out the notebook and said, "Would you mind jotting down your number? I'd like to repay you somehow and plus"—I pointed out the window—"let you know when the tractor will be removed."

He held up my card. "You know, I thought you looked familiar. I've read your articles in the paper." He grabbed the notebook and scribbled in it, then handed it back to me. "And don't mention it. That's what neighbors are for."

"How about I write a profile piece showcasing your work?"

"Sounds great."

And maybe I could find out more about what happened to his cousin.

They got Derek settled into the ambulance and I climbed in after him.

We passed Leo's car on White Hope Road.

He caught up with me at the hospital.

"Do I even want to know why you stole a tractor?" he asked me.

I was in the waiting area outside the emergency room flipping through a copy of *Guns and Ammo.*

"I didn't steal it, I borrowed it. I'll return it to Mr. Scoog."

"You going to return his bird too?"

That got my attention. "Liberty didn't go home?"

"Who is Liberty?"

"That's the name of the bird."

Leo sat down across from me and removed his sunglasses. His face was mostly tanned except for a slight strip where the bridge of the sunglasses covered his nose.

"All I know is that he tried to call you several times but it kept going straight to voice mail so he got the idea in his head that you ran off with his bird."

I chewed my lower lip. This was not good. I would feel absolutely horrible if something had happened to Liberty. After all, she may have saved both Derek's life and mine today.

It would be all my fault too.

I swore softly.

"Look, forget about the bird. I'm sure she'll turn up. And Gus brought the tractor back to the property. So"—he leaned forward—"are you going to tell me what happened?"

I met his gaze, trying to read his face. I couldn't tell if he was holding a busted flush or a full house.

I pretended to fumble through my bag for my phone, explaining that I was in the market for a scooter and I heard Mr. Scoog had the best deals in town.

Okay, I am not proud of the fact that I became a pathological liar, but I wasn't ready to show my cards to Leo yet.

Finally I felt it. I peeked to make sure the stone in my hand was the blue topaz I had been fishing for. It was. I was getting pretty good at recognizing the gems by touch since they were all different shapes and sizes. Not that I carried many in my workbag, but in my business, extracting the truth was important and blue topaz not only does this, but it aids in shedding light on uncertain situations. Since the path I was about to take with Leo was a dangerous one, or at the very least a stupid one, I needed all the help I could get.

I tried to tune him out for a moment as I focused on the question to the stone.

Topaz, blue and bright, what is his truth, where is my light?

"A scooter," Leo said. "Why was Derek with you?"

"He wanted a Coke machine. I hear they're collectable."

Leo nodded as if that made perfect sense. He must not have seen the one bullet that hit the tractor. At least not yet.

"Then what happened?"

"We got lost." I shrugged. "Look, it was scorching hot and we had very little water and that place is acres wide. And then Derek..."

Leo's face softened. "Then Derek got hurt."

He was offering his own explanation. His own theory. That was unusual for him, but great for me.

"So you panicked, saw the tractor, and went for help," Leo said, finishing the story.

From inside the bag, I squeezed the topaz hard in my hand. *Was this the right decision?* I didn't want to tell Leo anything yet for one reason and one reason only.

He would try to stop me from investigating my father's death. And in my mind, at that moment—while the topaz grew cold as ice in my palm—I knew it was murder.

I had my truth.

And no one was going to stop me from seeking justice.

No. One.

Chapter 17

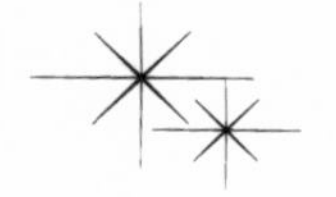

"Dogs are wise. They crawl away into a quiet corner and lick their wounds and do not rejoin the world until they are whole once more."

—Agatha Christie

A plump nurse wheeled Derek into the lobby. His leg was propped up and a big white boot had been slapped over his foot. "He'll probably be fine with some ibuprofen for the next couple of days, but we gave him Vicodin for now to ease the pain." She glanced at Derek, whose head rolled around on his neck. "Of course, he can't drive."

"I can take him home," Leo said. "Thank you, Sandy."

Leo went to sign some paperwork and I looked at Derek. "Hey, buddy, how are you?"

He smiled, a trail of spittle running down his cheek.

"I'm happy. Can we get ice cream?"

I knelt down, hands on my knees. "Sure we can. Hey, do you remember what happened today?"

"We saw a big bird. I like her. Where's the big bird?"

"Do you remember what else happened?"

If he let it all slip out, that would throw a huge wrench into my plan.

Derek smiled, then immediately frowned. His eyes widened and he said, "Oh yeah! We got sho—"

I covered his mouth with my hand and whispered in his ear. His eyes grew wide, he looked at his foot, and he passed out.

What can I say? A girl has to use every tool in her belt.

Leo strolled over and said, "All set. Did you want a ride to your car?"

"Nah, I'll help you get Sleeping Beauty tucked in and then if you could just drop me at the cottage, I would appreciate it." I had to get away from him before the enchantment faded away.

Leo hesitated. He looked at me as if he was forgetting something, but he shrugged it off, put his arms around me, and gently squeezed. "Glad you're okay."

"Thank you."

We eased Derek into the backseat and headed for his apartment. The manager let us in, since all his belongings were still back in my car. It didn't take long to get him all tucked in and I told Leo that I would come by and check on Derek later. Then he dropped me off at my place.

It had been hours since Thor was let out and he was ready to burst. In fact, he was pissed off that I left him home in the first place and told me by whizzing all over the porch.

"You know, sometimes you can be a real tool."

He harrumphed and ran off to investigate the shrubs.

I plugged my phone into the charger and checked my messages after I fed Thor his dinner. One was from Chance, saying he would pick me up at seven, there were three from Mr. Scoog, and one from Cinnamon telling me that there was a great band playing tonight and that I should stop by the Black Opal.

By the time I called Scoog back, Liberty had returned home unscathed and he wondered why his tractor was parked on the front lawn. I told him about Derek's foot injury and how it was difficult for him to walk and that seemed to smooth things over. He asked if Derek wouldn't mind stopping by for a playdate with Liberty sometime soon.

"She really seemed to take to that fella," Scoog said.

"I'll set it up," I said.

It was six o'clock when I poured my tired body into a bubble bath.

By seven, I was coiffed, fluffed, plucked, and ready to be wined and dined.

Of course, that's when I realized I'd forgotten to make the reservations.

I frantically dialed every nice eatery in town, from the French Bistro to the upscale Italian place with the white cloth table settings and the floating candle bowls.

"Sorry, we're all booked up" was the consensus.

My makeup was flawless, I was wearing my favorite little black dress with the rhinestone embellishment, red platform peep-toe heels, a silk shawl, and my hair was curled into a sexy updo.

Needless to say, I was not happy that the only place with an open table was Pearl's Palace, famous for its Friday night fish fry and rotating pie carousel.

"Don't worry about it," Chance said when he picked me up. He looked dashing in his gray suit and herringbone tie.

"I'm so sorry. It's been quite a day and I just didn't have the time."

Chance cocked one eyebrow at me as he drove down Main Street. "Well, you'll have to tell me all about it."

Where would I start?

I asked him to stop by Derek's before we went to the restaurant.

I hurried up the stairs to his apartment and was happy to find my coworker still sleeping soundly, so I rushed back to the car and Chance parallel parked into the first spot we found a few blocks from the restaurant.

Pearl of Pearl's Palace was a vivacious woman in her early sixties who kept her hair frosted, her nails painted, and her skirts frilly.

"Fancy seeing you here all dolled up, Stacy Justice." Pearl loved to say my full name and, truth be told, I liked the way her Texas twang made it sound like a song.

I leaned in for the double-cheek air kiss and said, "I don't suppose you have anything in a quiet corner?"

She winked at me. "Always keep something on hold in the back for romantic emergencies." She clasped my hands and whispered, "A dapper man like that should be enjoyed in private, am I right?" She looked at Chance and said, "Can you come by this week, sugar? I'm thinking of expanding my dining area and I need you to give me an estimate on tearing out that sad old counter."

Chance agreed.

Pearl escorted us past the Formica countertop with the chrome stools to a far-off table near a faux potted palm. A Chinese screen patched with duct tape provided privacy.

There was, however, a candle on the table so I couldn't really complain.

A waitress came over within seconds and Chance ordered a beer while I chose wine. The choice was red or white. I opted for white and had no doubt it came straight from a Franzia box.

Chance said, "Hey, how's the collie?"

"Fiona's keeping an eye on her until we can find her family. Still working on it, but she seems fine. I'll try to get her an appointment at the vet tomorrow."

"Great. Glad she's okay. So," he said and smiled warmly, "tell me about your day."

"You first." I caressed his hand.

Chance raised one eyebrow, but he didn't object. He just launched into the projects he had bid on today. A bathroom remodel, a condo update, a two-car garage with a loft overhead, and several smaller odd jobs.

"How about you?" He raised his beer for a toast and I met his glass with mine.

"Well, not a lot happened between the dead body and the sniper, but driving the tractor was fun." I took a large sip of wine.

Chance spit beer all over the potted palm. He studied me for a second. Either inspecting for bullet holes, signs of a concussion, or to gauge if I was pulling his leg.

He seemed to conclude that I was (a) unharmed and (b) completely serious.

"You want to take it from the top?"

I took a deep breath and gave Chance the highlights.

Thing was, Chance and I had an understanding. He didn't ask too many questions about my work, my family "obligations," or the string of dangerous situations and, let's face it, bad decisions both forced me into.

In return, I didn't lie to him. Heck, even if I wanted to, Chance had known me for too many years. He would see right through any baloney I could dish up.

That isn't to say I told him *everything*, because even I knew a man could take only so much.

For instance, the part about me being fully capable of breathing under forty feet of water? Omitted. The white tiger I spotted roaming around town? Completely glossed over.

When I finished, Chance leaned forward to say something, but the waitress appeared from behind the screen wall. She took our order and Chance waited until she was well out of earshot before he spoke.

"Okay, I understand that things..." The poor guy searched for the right word for like ten seconds, "...happen around you. I get that there are things I will never understand and that you may run across more dead bodies than a highway patrol officer." He paused and sipped some water.

"Why do I feel a 'but' coming?"

"However..." he said.

"Now see, that's just a *but* with more meat on it."

He flicked his eyes away for a moment.

Was he upset?

And to think I didn't even tell him everything.

"Stace, you aren't bulletproof."

"And you aren't sparkly. Now that we've both stated the absurdly obvious, what is your point?"

He set his napkin down and said calmly, "Okay, fine. I think you should tell Leo. All of it."

"I will." I sipped the wine. "As soon as I prove my father was murdered."

He cocked his head. "So you should get that wrapped up before the dessert tray comes, right?"

I stared at him hard. "Don't push me on this, Chance."

He sat back in his chair and just looked at me wistfully. This was not how I wanted the evening to go.

I had every intention of telling Leo about the shooter eventually, but I still hadn't fully checked out the car and I really wanted to search for those files. The caller made it a point to ask me about them—*you didn't find the files yet?*—which meant they were important. And since I was pretty sure the guy on the other end of the line was the same one I found in the lake, that was my only clue. I needed to copy them or at the very least make notes because if Leo got to them first they might be sealed as evidence and lost to me forever. Then I might never know what really happened all those years ago on that icy road.

Or who was responsible.

My best guess was that they were in the archives, and since Parker was fishing up north today, I had no way to access them. My key only opened the building and my office.

Chance ate his spaghetti in silence and I picked at my salmon, feeling like a jerk.

I set my fork down finally. "I just need tomorrow morning, okay? By lunchtime, I'll be at the police station. What's the harm in waiting a few more hours?"

This appeased him and we were able to salvage the rest of the evening with a shared chocolate mousse and a nightcap at the Black Opal. We were home before the band took the stage.

You know the expression "knock on wood"?

I should have.

Chapter 18

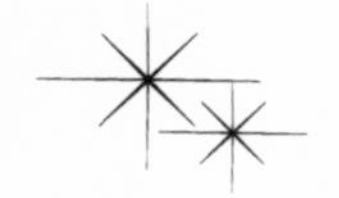

I woke up in Chance's arms when the alarm blasted at 6:00 a.m.

Sleepovers always sound like a great idea until I remember that the man I'm sleeping with keeps ungodly hours.

Chance turned the alarm off and kissed my forehead. Then my eyelids, then my lips. When he turned to roll out of bed, I grabbed him and pulled him close, interlacing my legs with his.

"I don't have much time." He rolled over to face me. "Don't want to start something I can't finish." His hair was tousled into a mess of sensual waves and his chin was covered in stubble.

"Oh, you'll finish." I climbed on top of him and proceeded to prove it.

After insisting he couldn't spend another minute in bed, Chance hopped in the shower and I climbed into an old T-shirt, shorts, and running shoes and went for a jog with Thor. On the walk back home, I gave Derek a call to see how he was doing and if he needed anything. No answer. Probably still asleep. I left a message saying I would pick him up for work.

When we returned, Chance was tossing his overnight bag onto the back bench of his truck. He was wearing a pair of faded, torn Levi's, work boots, and a white T-shirt. His hair was damp from the shower and there was just the slightest scent of the sea from the shampoo he used.

"Babe, I know I said I'd take you to get your car, but I can't be late for this hotel job. They want us out before three o'clock." He circled around the truck and gave Thor an ear scratch. "Think you can get Cinnamon or someone else to take you?"

I told him that shouldn't be a problem and he gave me a quick kiss before he hopped in and backed out of the driveway.

I ate some cereal, fed Thor, and took a quick shower. It was supposed to be another scorcher so I grabbed a gauzy skirt, a sleeveless green top, and strappy sandals to get ready for work. After dressing, I called Cinnamon for a ride. The bar closed at midnight on Sundays. I was hoping she had gotten enough sleep. My workday usually began at nine, and since there were still cars in the parking lot of the guest house, I figured Birdie and the aunts were cooking breakfast about now. Weekdays didn't bring a lot of guests, but with the Founder's Day Festival, we never knew who would stick around for an extra day or so.

Maybe Cinnamon could fill me in on Brian, the band member from the Hell Hounds. That vision of the man in the lake that hit me when I shook Brian's hand was still needling at the back of my mind.

What could it have meant? Did he know the man? What was the connection?

My cousin swung into the driveway, T-tops open on her Trans Am, a few minutes later. She looked livelier than she should have at that hour. She was wearing a blue tank top and cutoff shorts. She slipped her huge sunglasses on top of her head and grinned at me.

"Why are you cheerful?" I asked.

"You are looking at a well-rested woman." She flung her arm over the side of the door. "I wasn't feeling well last night so Tony closed up the bar and I got about ten hours of sleep."

Thor nibbled Cin's pinky finger as a greeting and hopped into the backseat. I put my workbag back there with him and we headed off toward the Junkyard Graveyard.

I casually mentioned Brian and she had nothing but high praise for the guy, which left me even more confused about the vision.

Then she said, "You going to tell me what's going on or do I have to read it in the paper?" She glanced sideways at me. "You do realize people blab about everything all over town and my bar is like the ten o'clock news."

I took a deep breath and unraveled the whole story, watching her expression as the words poured out. After a few minutes, Cinnamon pulled over and turned off the ignition.

"Why would anyone want to kill Uncle Stacy?"

"I don't know, Cin. But since I've got you, when we get there, maybe you could take a look at the car? Maybe there's some proof there that it was tampered with. If I bring Leo something substantial, he'll have to look into it."

"Sure, sure, sweetie. Whatever you need."

Cin started the car and pulled back onto the road.

Liberty was on her outside perch when we pulled up. She bobbed her head up and down and squawked as soon as I got out of Cin's car.

"I'll just wait to make sure the car starts." Cin cut her engine.

"Okay, just let me tell Mr. Scoog I'm picking it up. Be right back."

I hopped up the steps and tapped on the old man's door. "Mr. Scoog? It's Stacy Justice."

After a few seconds, I knocked again. "Mr. Scoog?" The door creaked open. "Hello?" I took a step inside and Liberty swooshed over my head, flapping her wings, then flew back out.

I turned and flashed Cinnamon a sign to say "just a moment."

She nodded. Thor was sitting upright in the backseat.

I hadn't been inside the trailer before. I was surprised to find it filled with boxes and boxes overflowing with paperwork stacked in no logical order that I could discern. I recalled Scoog saying he kept good records of any local wrecks. I guessed this is what that looked like after several decades.

"Mr. Scoog?"

No answer. Maybe he was out on the property? This wasn't a large home. Surely he would have heard me calling him.

I ducked into the kitchen. Nothing but a few empty beer cans and a half-eaten jar of Dinty Moore stew.

From the window over the counter, his backyard looked just as cluttered as the rest of the property. There was an old wheelchair propped next to a dilapidated outhouse, a few rusty bicycles, and a wind chime hanging from a plant stake.

I pulled out my cell phone and called the number he had called me from. A phone rang somewhere inside the trailer and I hung up after the third ring.

I decided to just grab the car and ask Leo to send a patrol to check on Mr. Scoog. If he was out on his property somewhere in this heat, there was no telling what could happen.

When I turned to head out, I noticed a spot of blood on the linoleum.

From the open door, Liberty screeched.

I stopped short, focusing all my energy on how my body felt in that moment. I stared at the red dot, which, come to think of it, could have been paint or ketchup.

No glaring signals, but there was a tickling at the back of my throat. Just the slightest hint of unease settled into my stomach. I wasn't sure how to read that. Usually my intuition was fine-tuned to protect myself and my circle, not strangers.

I scanned the floor, looking for more traces of red, but didn't find any.

What I did find, however, was a finger poking out from the corner of a dirty brown sheet sprawled across the sofa.

Silently I made a plea for the junk man to be sleeping peacefully.

I crept forward.

My voice cracked. "Mr. Scoog? You okay? You asleep?"

I watched for movement. Listened for wheezing.

Nothing.

I touched the finger. Still nothing, which was a good sign. No visions meant he wasn't dead.

"Mr. Scoog, I'm just going to lift up this sheet and make sure you're all right."

Deep breaths, Stacy. Deep breaths.

Tentatively I pulled the sheet back.

There was a pillow. Some folded blankets. A ledger.

No Mr. Scoog.

Just a limp, prosthetic arm.

Chapter 19

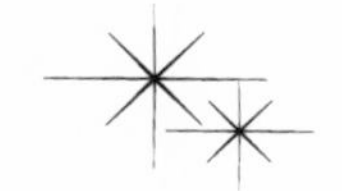

"Money will buy a pretty good dog, but it won't buy the wag of his tail."

—Josh Billings

This time, I called Leo directly and explained the situation. Cinnamon decided to wait with me for the chief to arrive, which was about ten minutes later.

"You know you really don't need to keep including me in these little adventures," she said.

"Very funny." I chewed my nail. "God, I hope he's all right."

"Oh sure," Cin said. "He's probably just at the casino playing the one-armed bandit."

I shot her a stern look.

"Too soon?"

Leo rolled up next to my car and I jogged around the side to his open window. "I still haven't seen—"

A tiny fur-covered rocket launched at my chest.

"Agh!"

Mini Thor was dancing up and down my shirt, shredding it in between growls and glares.

"Get this cockroach off me!"

Thor came charging out of the bushes, but Cin caught him by the collar in time and made him heel. He did so only out of respect, because I could see he was on point and ready to rumble and even Cinnamon wasn't strong enough to restrain my Great Dane in that agitated state. But after a few seconds of watching me wrestle with Satan's little helper, Thor cocked his head as if trying to comprehend the scene.

Or maybe he was choosing sides, I couldn't be sure.

Thankfully Leo was able to subdue my attacker, but not before my top took a beating.

I screamed at the Chihuahua, "Why do you hate me?"

Scrappy turned his back to me and cut wind.

"Calm down," Leo said. "Look." He put the dog in the car, fired up the air-conditioner, and rolled up the windows. He shut the door and faced me. "There. Won't happen again."

"Jesus, Chief, what the hell is that thing? Thor craps bigger than that," Cin said.

Leo said, "Forget about the dog. Walk me through what you saw."

After I composed myself, I did.

Leo checked out the trailer while Cinnamon and I waited. Thor was sniffing around the squad car, still trying to unlock the mystery of the four-legged fiend.

Liberty was flying around us, cawing incessantly when Leo returned. He was wearing a pair of gloves and in his right hand was a business card. My business card.

"I found this under his prosthesis."

"I gave that to him yesterday."

He flipped the card over, flashed it to me. "This mean anything to you?"

There were a slew of numbers and dashes that I couldn't comprehend at first.

But then I saw it.

The date my father died plus the make of his car and what appeared to be a vehicle identification number.

Perhaps Scoog had sifted through his records and scribbled the code on the back of my card to remember who I was and what brought me here.

Or maybe he was about to call to tell me about something he had discovered.

I revealed none of this to Leo. "Nope."

"Okay, I'll get a team together and we'll scour the property. I have to say, though"—he glanced back toward the trailer—"it doesn't look good."

That's what I was afraid of.

"You guys can go," Leo said.

"Will you let me know if you find him?"

Leo sighed. "Sure, but it could take hours."

Cinnamon scanned the property. "He pretty much kept to himself all alone out here, huh? Just him and the bird."

Leo nodded.

Wait a second.

Just him and the bird.

I said, "Leo, I have an idea."

Cinnamon left Thor with me and went home. I made a call to Derek, saying I would be a little late and then made the same call to Parker.

With all of her flapping and squawking, it became apparent that Liberty had been trying to tell us something all along, so it didn't take much coaxing for her to guide Leo to a thicket of overgrown raspberry and honeysuckle bushes. There, next to a pale yellow bucket dusted with a smattering of berries, lay Mr. Scoog.

There was no blood that I could see, which gave me some relief.

Leo bent toward him. Touched his wrist.

"He's dead," Leo said. He glanced around the area. "Looks like he was picking berries, maybe the heat got to him, he had a heart attack." Leo studied the scene.

"Why would he leave his arm behind to pick berries?"

The look on his face told me he was thinking the same thing. It also told me he didn't want me anywhere near another homicide.

"Maybe he was hot. Maybe he planned to shower after. The point is, right now, there appears to be no foul play."

He shoved my card inside his pocket and stepped away to make a phone call.

I took the opportunity to gain as much information as possible. I quickly drew a circle of protection, bathing in white light, as I crouched to touch Mr. Scoog's shoulder.

I closed my eyes. "Talk to me."

Abruptly he seized my hand, gripping me with the kind of fear that forces you to stifle a scream. My eyes shot open to find a black gaping hole where his glass eye had once been.

In his scratchy, cheerful voice he said, "Dead men tell no tales."

He laughed and collapsed back into the earth.

I yelped and took a tumble, shaking uncontrollably.

Thor came charging from behind a freezer chest to see what the hoopla was all about.

Leo spun around. He must have thought the dog had knocked me over because he said, "You all right?"

"I'm fine." I stood, dusted myself off. "Gotta get to work." I backed away, still shaking.

Leo had an oddly curious look on his face as he said, "Okay, then."

What. The. Hell. Was. That?

The dead had never spoken to me before. My messages came in dreams, gestures, images, but never anything verbal.

And what an eerie message it was.

Dead men tell no tales.

Or do they?

I jotted the words in my notebook as I watched Liberty fly back to her perch, looking a little less anxious than before, but sad nevertheless.

I wrote a note for Leo to call me later, adding that perhaps I could help place the bird and tiptoed to his car. The demon dog was sleeping soundly, so I clipped it beneath the windshield wiper.

A few minutes later, I tapped on Derek's door and he told me to come in.

He was trying to stabilize himself on one leg as he reached for his wallet.

I hurried over and snatched if off the table. He thanked me as I handed it to him.

"How are you feeling?" I asked.

He frowned. "This boot is a bitch to take a shower in and I can't even wear pants." He scanned the place, looking for something. "I can't find my camera shades. Did you take them?" He was patting himself down as if they might miraculously appear in one of the pockets on his cargo shorts.

"They broke, remember?"

He was still looking around the room. "Yeah, but I picked them up. They came with a warranty."

I raised my eyebrows. "Really? A warranty? Does that cover sniper attacks?"

He pointed at me. "About that. You need to fill me in on that noise. That was beyond off the hook. That was off the hook, on the ground, ripped and spillin' all over the floor."

"I have no idea what you're talking about."

Derek said, "It's a boxing metaphor, yo."

"I can't wait until you find a new girlfriend."

He just smiled.

"Okay, here's the deal."

I explained the whole story, from Saturday morning at the lake until today. The only tidbits I left out were the two dead guys animating in my presence.

"You're crazy, you know that?" Derek said when I told him that I failed to mention the gun-toting madman to Leo.

"It's only for today," I said quickly. "A couple of hours, Derek, until I can find those files the caller was talking about."

He hobbled over to the kitchenette. "You mean the dead guy in the lake."

"Right. At least I think that was who called me."

Derek grabbed a pair of sunglasses from the counter and put them on. "I won't lie for you."

I shook my head. "I'm not asking you to. I'm just asking you to lay low."

He considered this. "A couple hours. You swear?"

"Witch's honor." I grinned.

He took his shades off and pointed them at me. "That shit ain't funny."

"Fine. I swear."

He thought a moment and added, "I get the headlines."

"Deal."

I had him strapped into the car before I said, "Do you remember that bird?"

Chapter 20

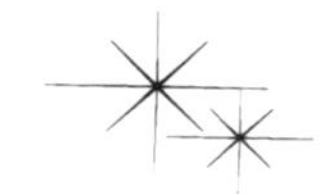

"Man is an animal that makes bargains: no other animal does this—no dog exchanges bones with another."

—Adam Smith

Derek wouldn't even discuss fostering Liberty. I dropped the subject as we pulled into the parking lot of the paper. We were already running late as we rushed directly into the conference room.

Well, I rushed, he hobbled.

Monday morning staff meetings were about as much fun as a radio without a dial. Today, however, was an exception because not only did we need to cover the Founder's Day Festival and our pathetic slaughter on the baseball field, but:

1. a homicide
2. the (suspicious) death of a town icon
3. the recovery of lost and formerly deceased canines

The town was buzzing and the phones were ringing due to the mysterious insurgence of canines. Gladys, our research assistant, had to turn on the answering machine just so she could keep up with recording the meeting minutes.

We went around the table discussing who would write which pieces for tomorrow's edition.

When I didn't volunteer for the headline stories, Parker's BS detector clicked into high gear.

"Wait a minute, Stacy." He shifted in his chair gingerly because he had a raging sunburn. "Are you telling me"—he paused and sipped some water—"that you found the body in the lake but you're passing the story to Derek?"

His red face was contorted in pain just from moving his lips. He looked like a lobster protesting its own execution.

"Well, Derek slept through most of the softball game. Someone has to cover it."

"Hey!" Derek said.

"I was going to take that myself," Parker said.

"You sure about that?" I asked. "You look like you need to take an aloe vera bath. Didn't you wear sunscreen on the ball field.

Parker winced as he picked up a pen. "I'm fine. It'll tan in a couple of days."

"Or it'll peel like a banana," I said. "Even your eyebrows look burned."

Iris Merriweather, the gossip columnist, said, "You should always wear sunscreen. Look at my face." She stuck her chin out and gave us a side-to-side profile view. "Sixty-five years old and not a darn wrinkle. I wear SPF seventy every day."

Gladys leaned in to inspect. I wondered what kind of fun house mirror Iris had at her place.

"Even I wear sunscreen," Derek said.

We all looked at him.

"You ever see skin cancer? It's ugly."

Parker was losing patience. "May we please get back to the assignments?"

"Okay, okay," I said. "Gladys, read what we have so far."

She clicked her dentures together and said in her thick Polish accent, "Yes. I have here..." She flipped back a few pages and perched her blue reader glasses on her nose. "Body Discovered in Eagle Lake—Derek. Founder's Day Happenings—Iris. Softball Game—Mr. Parker. I have no one for doggies."

"I'll take that one," I said. "One of the dogs is at the inn. A gorgeous collie. No one has claimed her yet."

Parker looked at me. "Really? What about Thor?"

At the sound of his name, Thor stood up and rested his bowling-ball-sized head on the table. Iris gave him a pat on his black muzzle.

"That's why she's not at my place, but the Big Man has been told to keep his distance." I narrowed my eyes at Thor, who sneezed all over the meeting minutes.

Parker did a scan of the table. "So we're good? What about Mr. Scoog?"

"How did you know about that?" I asked.

Iris said, "I told him. Ran into Amy, the new dispatcher, at the coffee shop. Cute little thing." Iris also owned Muddy Waters, the town's source for caffeine and sugary pastries.

Derek said, "Oh yeah? How cute?"

"Okay, team." Parker pulled his chair back. "Meeting adjourned."

His body was stiff as he did a John Wayne walk out of the room.

We all filtered out and I asked Derek to take Thor into his office so I could catch up with Parker.

A few minutes later I was seated across from my boss in a comfy brown leather chair, wondering where to begin this conversation.

"What's up, kiddo?" he asked.

I told him about the phone call on Friday, about the likely connection between that call and the man pulled from the water. He told me Leo had asked him about a phone call.

I asked, "Do you know what he meant about the tapes?"

Parker thought for a moment, scratched his chin, and instantly regretted it. "Ow." He said, "That was a long time ago. I don't remember what your father was working on."

"Did he seem nervous at all? Did he mention anyone threatening him?"

Parker looked off in the distance for a moment. "No. That I would remember."

I stared down at the floor. There had to be something here. Some connection.

Parker leaned across his desk. "Stacy, that phone call was probably from some crackpot. I mean, how do you know for certain it came from the man in the lake? Heck, we get calls like that all the time."

He reached into a ceramic box shaped like a treasure chest and pulled out a bottle of aspirin. "I know it might be easier to seek blame somewhere, but sometimes an accident is just an accident." He popped a couple of pain relievers and washed them down with water. "Besides, we have other stories to cover right now."

It was no accident, but I didn't know how to convince Parker of that. Sure, if I spent time chasing this down it would cut into my work, but there was a bigger story here. And if I cracked it, Shea Parker would be the first one congratulating me.

I stood up and walked over to a photo of the two of them holding an award.

I was twelve years old the first time my father brought Parker home for dinner. Even then, I could see the man was a contrast to my dad. Dad was a bold, confident soul who played until his muscles were sore and worked until his fingers bled.

Shea was polite but cautious, always leaving a sip in the glass and food still on the plate.

For a man who didn't like to upset the applecart, he sure picked the wrong family to build a business with.

I turned to face him. "I'm not a little girl anymore, Shea. I'm a hungry reporter with a seething need in my gut to follow this thing, wherever it may lead. So if I have to work twenty-four seven on this, I will. With or without your help."

Parker sighed and sat back in his chair. He winced, either from the sunburn or my stubbornness; I couldn't be certain. He stood up, joined me at the photograph, and just stared at it for a moment. Finally he said, "He was the first person I met when I came here from Madison. It's hard to blend into a small town." He adjusted the picture. "All it took was one beer and a friendship was born. People said we were crazy to go into publishing, but your dad, he didn't let the naysayers get to him. He had gumption. And everything he touched turned to gold." He sighed. "What do you want me to do?"

"His files."

He looked at me funny for a moment and not just because of the sunburn.

"What?"

"Stacy, all his files were destroyed five years ago when the basement flooded."

Chapter 21

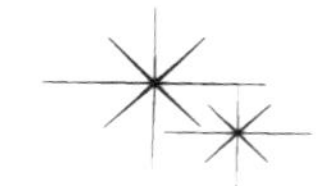

"Life is like a dog sled team. If you ain't the lead dog, the scenery never changes."

—Lewis Grizzard

Just one freaking time I would like to have a banner day where everything goes according to plan.

This was not that day.

At my insistence, Parker escorted me to the archive room, and sure as Shinola, it was empty.

I tossed my head back and yelled, "Dammit!" I ran my fingers through my hair and took a deep breath. "Well, at least I can go through the soft copies of the articles he wrote around that time."

Parker was unusually quiet. He studied a crack in the concrete.

"Don't tell me—"

He wrinkled his forehead and frowned. "I don't know where he kept his personal backups. He took disks home every night, but the main files we collected from his desk after his death were stored in the basement."

I wanted to punch something. So I did.

Parker doubled over and said, "Ow. That was uncalled for."

"Well." I looked around at the empty basement. My father had to have left some trace of his work. Maybe Birdie would know where? "I guess I'll get to work on the dog story."

I spent a couple of hours calling back the numbers left on the answering machine from stunned pet owners. After several interviews, I wrote the story, including a profile of Keesha. Gladys drove Derek to the inn to snap a photo of her to run alongside the text in hopes that someone would recognize the pretty pooch. I didn't know if the dog had been stolen, but it was one scenario since no one had claimed her yet.

Then I made a quick call to the vet—prompted by one of the interviewees, who explained that his dog had been microchipped for the express purpose of identifying the pup if he ever got lost. Apparently it was some sort of chip inserted into the dog's skin that, when scanned, would show up in a database that held the family's contact information.

Hopefully some good would come out of this disastrous weekend. The thought that perhaps I may have at least saved an innocent dog from Goddess knows what gave me some comfort.

Some. Not much.

I was edgy, anxious, and I didn't know where to focus that energy. My office wasn't exactly spacious, but I stood up and paced it anyway after I sent the piece to Parker. What next? It was driving me absolutely crazy that there were no leads in my father's death. There was no proof that it was murder, but surely the messages, the visions—the dead men talking—weren't all for naught.

The sun shone through the window brightly at this time of day and my attention was drawn to the far wall where the three muses sword hung. The gift from Birdie was embedded with tiny crystals that refracted the light brilliantly, splashing miniature rainbows across the wall.

I shuffled over Thor and put my hand on the hilt, receiving an instant static shock. I yanked away for a second. My eyes were drawn to the inscription on the blade. *The Divine lies in these three: Justice, Knowledge, Mercy.*

I gripped it with both hands and flipped it over to read the back.

Follow your instincts. Trust in your power. Defend your honor.

I set off to do just that.

I grabbed Thor's travel bag and loaded it into the car. Thor hopped into the backseat and I rolled all the windows down. Then I drove to Muddy Waters coffee shop on Main Street. They had a great selection of premade salads and sandwiches, and since I had other plans for my lunch hour, I didn't want to waste it waiting for my food to be prepared.

The veggie panini looked good in the glass case so I chose that along with a couple of bottles of water. Iris was already there helping with the lunch crowd. I was just about to pay her when I heard Cinnamon call my name.

I turned to see her sitting at a round glass table supported by old Singer sewing machine stands. She was sitting next to Brian from the Hell Hounds and, I assumed, his band members. My cousin waved me over.

I pasted a smile on my face, recalling the image I received when I shook Brian's hand. "Hi there."

Cinnamon said, "This is my cousin, Stacy."

Brian said, "We met yesterday. How are you feeling?"

The question came with concern. There was no malice that I could measure from him.

"Fine, thanks." I held up my sandwich bag. "Just getting a quick bite."

Cin said, "Why don't you join us?"

A woman with a skull tattoo on her back and a shock of white hair with trails of black running through it was sitting in front of me. She didn't turn around as she said, "You should." She put her hand on Brian's knee, indicating that he was her property.

"Actually, I can't." I tilted my head toward the door. "Thor's waiting for me."

Brian said to one of his bandmates, "Man, you have to see this dog. He's as big as a horse."

The guy was somewhere in his forties with spiky hair that I guessed hadn't changed since Billy Idol dominated the rock charts. His eyes were red and hazy as he said, "Yeah, I remember a big dog right before the gig." He nodded as if the event had happened in years past rather than a few days ago.

A fourth band member pulled up a chair and nodded at me. He looked more like an accountant than a rocker. "These bathrooms here are cleaner than any I've ever been in." He unscrewed the cap on a bottle of Perrier and sipped.

I wanted to stick around just to get some information, but Thor was waiting for me and I had at least one other stop to make before I went back to work. Plus, it was only a matter of time before Leo caught up to me.

"How long are you guys in town?" I asked.

"We're taking off tomorrow," Brian said.

Cinnamon said, "They'll be playing again tonight. Stop by the bar."

I said I would and hurried out the door.

Leo texted me just as I pulled past the thick wrought-iron gates of the cemetery.

We need to talk.

I texted back. *K. Be there ASAP.*

I powered the phone off, stuffed it in my pocket, and grabbed a blanket from the trunk.

Thor and I followed the meandering gravel path past a statue of the Virgin Mary holding baby Jesus. The headstones near the front of the grounds were so old the names and dates had weathered away from years of being battered by rain, snow, sleet, and hail. Some of the stones had partially crumbled into the earth. Others, mostly those from the last few decades, were carved from shiny marble or heavy granite. Fresh flowers had been sprinkled throughout the landscape—roses, daisies, gladiolas. Occasionally I came across a grave with a potted palm or a fern. Remembrance offerings from loved ones.

It took ten minutes for Thor and me to reach my father's gravesite.

It was easy to spot when we did because the regal tiger was sprawled across it. As we grew closer, she melted away.

"No, wait! Mom!"

But it was too late. She was gone.

I didn't know how my mother was transporting her spirit guide to me from the Old Country, or if she was somehow sending me the illusion of one, but when I saw the ghostly beast there, I knew that my mother was attempting to communicate with my father.

Had she succeeded?

And if she had, what was she telling him?

Thor sat down next to me, leaning just a bit, and panting.

"Come on, boy."

There was a towering oak nearby and I set his dishes up beneath it, then filled them with food and water. He got busy slurping up the refreshments and I shook the blanket out and laid it on my father's resting site. I pulled out a penny and placed it on the smooth, gray stone. My offering.

"Hi, Dad. I know I haven't visited in a while." I unwrapped the sandwich and took a bite, searching for the words. The vinegar dressing was both bitter and sweet gliding down my throat. "I guess it seems silly to sit here because I can talk to you anywhere, really. Birdie says the departed are never far from us." Clouds tumbled in overhead, offering a bit of relief from the heat. "Then again, Birdie says a lot of things."

A cardinal fluttered past and landed on the neighboring tombstone. His crimson head stretched toward the sky as he sang into the wind. I stared at him for a moment, thinking that his life was beautifully simple and wishing I had that kind of peace. The peace from knowing that you could always find shelter from a storm by building a sturdy home. That your family would be safe as long as you kept an eye out for predators.

Except there were always predators.

"I need your help on this one, Dad. I need your guidance to find out what happened to you." I considered for a moment dipping into my herbs and crystals and casting a spell to call him. But a cemetery is filled with a full spectrum of energy—good, bad, mischievous.

Evil.

Sacred burial ground is a powerful source for enchantments and I wasn't confident that my state of mind was sturdy enough to contain the charm to just my father.

The last thing I needed was a park full of dead people hitching a ride home with me.

I nibbled at my sandwich again, wrapped up the remainder, and put it in my satchel.

Wild nettle grew along a nearby fence line. I picked some of that, thanking the gods for planting it there, and dusted it all around my father's resting place for protection.

I waited for a sign that he was near. A whisper in the wind. A butterfly passing over the penny. Any indication that he could communicate with me.

None came.

Finally I stood, cleared the space, and cast a second circle of protection all around me.

On my knees, I made a triangle with my hands and brought them to my chest. After several deep breaths, I closed my eyes and imagined pushing out all the thoughts. The brain chatter formed into visual words with legs, the images became photos, and I took a wide-brushed broom and swept it all aside. I tossed my emotions on top of the pile—love, anger, fear, sorrow—one by one. Next, I pictured a large door at the edge of my mind. When I opened it, all the clutter tumbled out. I slammed it shut and locked it with a big brass key.

The last step to opening up completely to whatever may come was several more tapered breaths.

Then I waited.

A few minutes later, my dad walked into the white room of my mind's eye, a folded newspaper tucked under his arm. He sank into a large brown leather chair. Seconds after, another man stepped into the room, younger. He sat in an identical chair across from my father and produced a beer bottle, which he uncapped. Then, out of nowhere, that damn Chihuahua bounded into the room, but before I could shoo him out, the trance was broken by the piercing ring of my stupid cell phone.

My eyes popped open. I reached into my bag, about to answer the call. Then I remembered.

I had turned it off.

I checked the screen.

Black as ink.

But still ringing.

Chapter 22

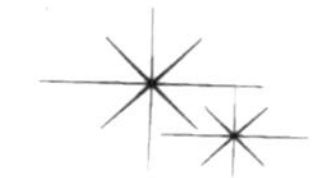

I was still on my knees when I lifted the phone to my ear.

"H-hello?"

The reception was scratchy, like an untuned radio dial.

"Dead men tell no tales." Mr. Scoog's voice.

After that, the same voice from the call the other day. "Your father was murdered." He repeated it over and over again until I couldn't stand it any longer.

I screamed, dropped the phone, and danced away from it.

Right out of my circle of protection.

Uh-oh.

They came at me not in a wave, but in pockets. Clusters of people—spirits—grouped together by I don't know what. Families? Time of death? Hair color?

The first to reach me was a blonde woman in a beaded black flapper dress with so much kohl eyeliner I wondered if she used actual coal. A man wearing a fedora stood next to her looking confused. The woman seemed a little drunk.

"Listen, doll," she said, rushing at me. "Tell my great-great-granddaughter that I'm proud as all get out!"

The man said, "And how!" Then he looked around and added, "Say, where's the hooch?"

Oh, this was not happening. "I, I don't know your great-great-granddaughter."

The woman waved her arm. "Sure you know her, honey. You live here in town, don'tcha? Everybody knows everybody in this backwater burg. Isn't that right, Dash?"

Dash had wandered off already, apparently looking for the hooch. Thor was fighting his way through the crowd, trying to get to me. He learned quickly that his impressive frame and go-to intimidation tactics would not work on this bunch.

"Name's Fontaine, honey, Monique Fontaine!" She sauntered off in search of Dash, her beads clicking together with every sashay of her hips.

Oh no. No. No. This was not in the cards. I did not want to be bound by some ancestral oath to deliver messages all over town to descendants of the deceased.

I backed up into the circle of nettle and bumped into a fluttering, nervous energy. A waif of a man was chewing on his nails and sputtering at me. His black hair fell over his eyes and he had a rope around his neck.

"I didn't mean to do it. Please tell my mother I didn't mean to do it. The chair slipped. I was…trying to…you know…" He made an obscene hand gesture and I almost vomited.

Two Civil War soldiers, one Confederate, one Union, were standing right behind him, patiently waiting their turn. The Confederate soldier said, "Sir, you are frightening this woman. Kindly step aside."

The small man turned on him like a rabid animal and both soldiers drew their swords.

"What battalion are you from?"

The hanged man scattered to the wind.

"Ma'am, we have but one request," said the Union soldier. He flicked his eyes to the Confederate soldier. "My brother and I would like to know who won the battle."

My voice was shaky. "I don't know which battle you are referring to, but I can tell you who won the war."

Their eyes grew large. Neither could have been over eighteen years old when they died. They looked at each other for a split second and both tightened their grips on their weapons.

"But only if you promise to stop fighting."

Reluctantly the swords found their way into the sheaths.

"The North."

The Union soldier jumped up and down and said "Ha!" to his brother.

The Confederate soldier looked defeated. So I said, "I'm pretty sure Grant was hung over when Lee surrendered. He was also covered in mud, his uniform was rumpled, and he hadn't bathed in a while by all accounts."

"Undignified swine," said the teenager in gray. They both marched off.

There was a commotion in the crowd behind me as a fistfight broke out.

"Stop that!" I yelled.

Thor charged toward the hoopla and a man with a goatee held his hands up. "Not again!" he screamed and ran the other away.

The man he was fighting said, "It was a Rottweiler got him last time. Serves him right for breaking into that house in the first place when the kids were home. Hit an empty pad, that's what I always say." Then he lit a cigarette and said, "Listen, I got a job for my cousin—"

A large black woman in a housecoat with a yellow scarf tied in her hair cut him off. "Not in my house, son." Her voice carried a Southern twang. "God-fearing people go before scumbags." She had at least a hundred pounds on him. Maybe two.

"You don't even live here," the man protested.

She didn't? I thought.

She moved forward with the determination of a mother bear, parked her hands on her generous hips, and stared him down.

He shrugged and said, "I got time." The man leaned against a headstone and puffed on the smoke.

The large woman turned her attention back to me. "Darlin', I want you to tell my grandnephew to get his butt back to law school. His grandmomma is all up in arms about him quittin' and she won't stop prayin' and yappin' to me. I got things to do, you know? Just cuz I'm dead don't mean I aint livin'. Can't be called to her side every time she needs a favor, but then again, Maybel was always a drama queen. Do you know that one time she—"

"Pardon me, but what is his name?"

The interruption perturbed her, but the energy in the air was growing hostile and I didn't want another argument to break out. Although I couldn't believe I asked the question, because I certainly had no intentions of following through with the request.

She smiled and said proudly, "Derek Meyers. Fine-lookin' boy and smart as a whip! Won the state spellin' bee back in..."

I stopped listening. Derek had been in law school? Well, this kept getting better and better. Geez, I really hoped there was no penalty for not following through with these deliveries. I mean, what the hell was I supposed to say? *Hey, Derek, you know what the world needs? More lawyers.* I certainly couldn't tell him the truth. Although he did have an aunt in New Orleans who was a voodoo priestess. Maybe I could just tell him she called to relay this message.

"Got it," I said.

"Hmm-hmm." She adjusted her scarf, nodded, and faded into a mist.

That was when I spotted a group of children playing tag a car's length away. A thin woman with long, straight hair stood in the center of them looking like a wild animal caught in a trap.

Something about her eyes drew me to her.

Thor followed and the kids swarmed the dog, squealing with delight, galloping all around him and high-fiving each other. Of course, the big ham welcomed the attention.

The crowd was multiplying around me, shouting requests, and my nerves began to bubble. I centered my focus on the woman, trying to block the noise, but I could feel a vein pulsating in my forehead.

The stench of burned rubber mixed with something metallic seeped from her.

She didn't meet my eyes as she spoke. "I heard it, you know. Just before." Her hands fidgeted with the buttons on her floral blouse. "But there was no time." Her voice was shallow and a sob escaped her throat as the tears fell.

My heart twisted into knots at the pain she must have felt.

"I don't know what went wrong. It wasn't supposed to be there." She looked at me questioningly. "I stopped. I did, I know I did." Her eyes were raw with emotion.

I nodded in empathy.

"But the kids"—she trailed her gaze to them, watched as Thor joined in the chase game—"they were singing some stupid song. 'Old MacDonald,' I think it was." She called to one of the little ones, told him not to climb a tree. "It was the first day of school, so I thought, let them have fun. Just be kids." She wiped her eyes with the back of her hand, shook her head, and said, "It wasn't supposed to be there."

"You're right," I said. "It wasn't. It was a new route they were trying."

Her eyes fell on me and there was a spark of hope behind the moisture. She wrinkled her brow. "Really? Because I stopped, I swear I did. I looked, but I didn't see it. Do they know that?" She searched my face for an answer. "The parents, I mean. Do they know I stopped?"

"They know. It was an accident. That's all. Just an accident."

She nodded, looked down at the well-manicured grass. "So senseless. So much lost and for what?" Her shoulders sagged with the weight of her burden.

"One good thing came from it."

She looked at me skeptically. "What could that possibly be?"

"After the accident, the town got a grant from the state. The Federal Highway Act of 1973 urged every state to inspect each crossing, but it was a slow process. The accident allowed for the town to be granted the funds to install gates, bells, and flashing lights."

"Really?" A small smile crept across her face. "Do you think that helped?"

"It saves lives."

"Oh." She looked at the children. "That makes me happy." She turned and suddenly threw her arms around me. "Thank you," she whispered.

The electricity of her touch jolted through me like lightning. Her entire life and death flashed before my eyes, and when she finally released me, I felt as if I had just taken a shower with a toaster.

I wobbled for a moment as she whisked off toward the kids.

That's when I heard the words that changed my life forever. "We can touch her?"

Holy Moses and his brother Doug. This was not good.

Arms and voices came at me in all directions and my heart rate jumped into overdrive.

"No, no. Please. One at a time!"

The faces and voices collided into a terrifying wave of desperation. My own desperation was bleeding through as I searched for an escape route.

There was none.

"Thor!" I cried, but I didn't see or even hear him.

My throat began to close up and I realized I was having a panic attack. I thought I spotted the man from my meditation, but I couldn't be certain.

"People, calm down, please!"

Just then, I heard a gunshot. I twisted my neck to see a one-armed man fire again.

"Back off! This little lassie needs her space."

The voice was familiar. But he looked too young. “Mr. Scoog?”

He winked his glass eye at me.

Someone shouted, “He’s a newbie! He hasn’t even gone through registration yet!”

Wow. Even in death, there was paperwork.

Someone disarmed Scoog and the mob turned their sights back to me.

I stretched my arms out to distance them. It was about as effective as herding cats with a laser pointer.

“Can you tell my husband that skank he married is cheating on him?” one woman asked. “The rat bastard.”

A round man said, “Tell my son the family sauce recipe is hidden behind the painting of his uncle. No more of that canned crap!”

“Sure, sure.”

I backed away as they hurled more and more demands. They kept moving forward, reaching, groping, vampiring my life force. My heart was beating so fast, I was sure it would explode.

My last thought, before I tripped over a tree root and took a header into a headstone, was, *How ironic would it be to die in a cemetery?*

Chapter 23

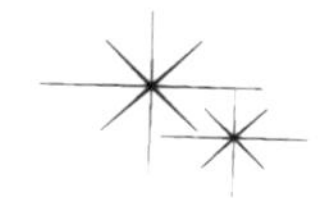

"Yesterday I was a dog. Today I'm a dog. Tomorrow I'll probably still be a dog. Sigh! There's so little hope for advancement."

—Snoopy

The pungent aroma of frankincense awakened me.

There were voices. Questioning voices that made me hesitate to open my eyes.

Please, please don't let me see dead people.

I heard the cardinal's song and a familiar woman said, "Hello, Mr. C, nice to see you." She punctuated her greeting with her own whistle to the bird.

Fiona was here.

But where was here? Slowly I opened my eyes.

The three Geraghty Girls were huddled over me all suited up as if they were hosting a sporting event for sorcerers and I was the crystal ball.

"She'll be fine now," Birdie said and stepped back.

I sat up, looked around. I was back on top of my father's grave, ensconced in a circle of candles, herbs, and gemstones. Thor had his head in my lap, looking worried. My legs had fallen asleep from the weight of it.

"It's a good thing your familiar was smart enough to call on us," Birdie said. Her crimson cape flared around her and she was wearing so much jewelry, her neck wasn't visible.

"Thanks, Thor." I kissed his big black nose.

He yawned and hauled himself to his feet. I shook out my legs.

A phone rang and I jumped. It was in Lolly's hand and I said, "Don't answer that!"

Too late. Lolly picked it up and said, "Hello? Hello? Who's this, please?"

She shrugged and said, "This thing is fussy." Then she handed it to Fiona.

"You were holding it backward, dear," Fiona said. "Hello? Yes, Stacy is right here." Fiona reached her hand out, her emerald cape covering all but her rose-colored manicure.

I shook my head, "Take a message."

I wasn't falling for that crap again.

Fiona shrugged and said, "Mr. Parker, she isn't feeling well right now. May I take a message?" She paused. "Well, I'm not sure, I think perhaps she may need the afternoon off." Another pause. "Yes, of course. Bye-bye." She clicked the phone off and said, "I guess it was a good thing Lolly turned it back on. He had a question about an article you submitted."

Thank you, gods.

Lolly leaned in to grab the phone and her yellow cape parted just enough to reveal a Wonder Woman costume complete with red satin boots and golden lasso.

Which explained the headband.

Fiona said, "Do you mind if she uses it, dear? Lolly likes the Texas Hold 'Em app."

"So," Birdie said, her words sharp as razors, "would you care to explain?"

I sighed and rose to my feet. Still a bit shaky, I touched my father's stone for support.

"Okay, let's go."

The three of them exchanged glances and Birdie said, "No. Here. Now."

It was not up for debate.

I was too weak to argue anyway. I began with the phone call, which led to the visions, the dead guy in the water, the tiger sightings (and what I thought they signified), the shooting, Mr. Scoog, and the meditation. I ended with the grand finale of being accosted by a bunch of spirits all seeking some form of closure.

I wiped a trace of sweat from my brow and felt a lump on my skull beneath a bandage. Birdie must have patched my head where it smacked the granite. My bag was in a heap within the circle and I reached for it to grab a water.

Lolly quickly slapped my hand away. She handed me a leather flask. I took a swig and spit out the stinging liquid.

"Is that tequila?"

Lolly frowned and said, "Sorry, that's mine." She reached into her cape and produced a second flask. "Detoxifying tea."

I sipped it. Tasted a lot like Earl Grey.

The three of them huddled again, whispering.

They broke out of it a few minutes later. Lolly and Fiona looked a bit too excited for my liking.

Birdie was wearing her poker face, but I could see she wasn't as angry as I thought she would be.

Which scared the bejesus out of me.

"We think the tiger is your mother's messenger sent to protect you."

"Not her?"

Birdie said, "Impossible. Her astral force would be bound to her confines by the terms of her punishment."

Fiona chimed in, "But she learned to wield her guides well. Her gift of predicting harm to you, it seems, has returned." Fiona smiled. "That, my child, bodes well."

"For what?"

"For her retrieval." Birdie couldn't help but grin. "When you go before the council this Samhain, we expect them to rule in our favor."

I clasped my hands together. "Birdie, that is wonderful news. However, right now, I've got a few other things to worry about."

Birdie nodded. "Tell us about the meditation."

I explained in detail exactly what I did and who appeared—my father, the other man, and of course the four-legged intruder that I met at the park after my spell. They huddled together again, which pissed me off, but I bit my tongue.

I heard Fiona say, "Of course it's the same dog. Odd, him coming back."

"What dog? Who are you talking about?"

Fiona turned around and said, "Your first familiar, of course."

Oh hell no. Oh no, no, no.

"Wait a second, time out, time out, team!" I made a T with my hands. "Are you telling me that nasty little gnat that did this"—I pointed to my scratched-up shirt—"was my dog at one time?"

Fiona frowned and said, "Honestly, sweetheart, I can take you shopping for new clothes. You went to work like that?"

I felt that vein in my forehead again. "Focus, please. Explain." I snapped my fingers.

Fiona stepped away from her sisters and told me about the adorable little Chihuahua she got me when I was two years old.

"But that doesn't make any sense. I don't remember him."

"Well, you were so upset by his passing that I took care of that," my great-aunt said.

This was a nightmare. That rodent was once my familiar? It couldn't be. It just couldn't. Unless...

I hated to ask, but I had to know. "Fiona, can you think of any reason why he would be angry with me?"

She said, "No, not really," and turned back to her sisters. After a beat, she popped her head out of the circle and said, "Except, of course, you killed him."

"What? Did not!"

What a horrible thing to say. Until I met him, I never even had a bad thought about an animal.

"You left the gate open, dear. That's why the car hit him. He never matured into his full potential as a familiar. Which means he cannot evolve into a spirit guide. It was all he ever wanted," she said sadly.

I was stunned. Stunned. "Well, but…how old was I?"

She tilted her head toward the sky and said, "Oh, about four, maybe five."

Okay, I didn't feel so bad, but still. I had amends to make.

And I was not looking forward to it.

It seemed an eternity had passed and I was sprawled on the ground beneath a maple, using Thor's behind as a pillow when they approached.

"We have something to tell you," Lolly said.

I put my hands over my eyes to shield out the sun. "What is it?"

Birdie cleared her throat. "It seems conclusive to us that Stacy Senior met with foul play."

Just like that. Said it like she was ordering lunch.

I laid there for the longest time, absorbing the strength of the women around me, recharging my wares from the spirits who had stolen my energy, and just listening to the even breathing of my dog.

An odd peace came over me. An acceptance.

It was true. My father was murdered. It wasn't my dream that led to his death after all.

Which meant I had turned my back on my family, my heritage, my calling—for nothing.

I banged my fist on the ground and felt a fire leap inside me. It would fester there for days to come.

But right then, something broke. Something altered within me.

It is difficult to describe the moment when you realize the person you are is not the same as the person you must become to face the challenges before you. It's a slithery, uneasy sensation like a tarantula shedding its skin.

But victory only comes with sacrifice.

And failure was not an option.

It was time. Time to let go of the fear.

Time to become who I was born to be.

I rose to my feet and said, "Teach me."

The Geraghty Girls stopped chattering for a moment and stared at me.

"Teach you what, dear?" Fiona asked.

I looked from her, to Lolly, to Birdie. "How to be the Seeker of Justice."

Chapter 24

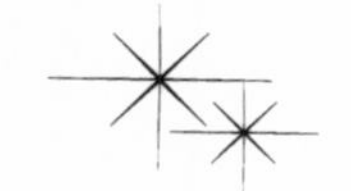

"Some of my best leading men have
been dogs and horses."
—Elizabeth Taylor

My initial lesson was to begin tonight, but I had much to do before then. I dropped Thor off at home and then called Parker back.

"Hey, I was just fact checking your article and these dates can't be right. Some of these dogs were lost for, like, fifteen years."

"According to the pet owners, they're right."

Pause. "Maybe I should run the piece without the dates."

"Probably not a bad idea."

We disconnected, and Chance called, telling me he would be working late. I told him I had plans with Birdie and that I would be at the Black Opal later if he wanted to meet me there.

I was on my way to the police station to talk to Leo when a thought occurred to me so I called Fiona. Before we parted ways, she had provided me with some tips on what to do with the pissed-off pup.

I said, "I understand what I'm supposed to do with the incantation, but how do I explain to Leo what happened to the dog?"

"One cannot remember what was never there."

Right.

I double-checked my pocket for the charm after I pulled into the parking lot.

A young girl stood behind the reception desk when I walked through the doors.

She looked up, smiled. "Hi, Stacy, I'm Amy. I recognize you from your picture in the paper."

As Iris said, she was a cute little thing who looked more like a woodland sprite than a dispatcher. She had a fluff of blonde curls with pink skin and sparkly eyelashes.

"Hi, Amy, is Leo here?"

"Gee, you just missed him. He got called out to the Shelby Farm."

"What was it this time?" The high school kids were forever playing pranks on Mr. Shelby. Summer in a small town meant they had very little to keep them entertained.

"They glued magnets to the goats and now they're all sort of stuck to the fence."

I said, "Well." Because there was no other response for that.

"Gus is here if you want to talk to him. You can go on back."

"Thanks, Amy."

I found Gus at his computer registering for ComicCon.

"Oh, hey, Stacy. The chief isn't here."

"I know, Gus."

His focus went back to the screen.

"Hey, where's that adorable little dog? Thought maybe I'd take him for a quick walk."

"That would be great. Leash is on the door. He's sleeping in Leo's office. It's not locked."

"Great."

I grabbed the leash and steeled myself for an attack.

As promised, mini-Thor was sleeping soundly in a tiny round bed beneath Leo's desk. He must have smelled me before he saw me because his nose twitched. Fiona said for the enchantment to work properly, it would be best if I took him back to the area where I found him.

I whispered, "Thor."

Felt weird to call another dog that. Especially one the size of a peanut.

He opened one eye. Took one look at me and growled, his teeth vibrating between his lips.

I was afraid of that.

"Thor, old friend. Listen to me."

He opened the other eye, stood up, and stretched. He put his head down low and pinned his ears back.

"I know you're upset, but I'm here to make it up to you."

If he had been launched from a slingshot, he couldn't have hit me harder.

"Calm down, calm down!"

He clamped onto my boob and I cried out. I kicked the door shut while trying to wrestle him off me. "Shh!" He snapped and spit, strong for such a tiny thing. It was like trying to fight off a Venus flytrap.

"Fiona! Remember Fiona?"

He stopped mid snarl and cocked his head.

"That's right, Fiona. She gave me something that will make it all better. But you must trust me. Okay?"

He looked skeptical.

"Look, I am really, really sorry that I ruined your dream. But if you let me, I'll make it right."

He grunted for good measure and jumped down.

I quickly got him in the car before he changed his mind.

There were a few kids at the park, so we took the long route down to the pet cemetery. Mini-Thor kept a pretty good pace while keeping one eye on me as if I might double-cross him any moment.

We found the little grave with his name on it next to a fern patch.

I took the leash off him and said, "Again, I apologize for my carelessness. I was just a kid."

He barked once.

"Come." I pointed to the place where he should sit, at the center of his burial spot.

He followed my direction and sat facing north. Then I extracted one black ribbon, to release him of the spell I put out Saturday night, one red, representing that he was once a familiar, and one white, to send him on his journey to become a spirit guide.

I took them all one by one and charged them with my requests, first by placing them on my third eye and then via the sun's rays.

That done, I tied the three ribbons together.

"Cernunnos, guardian of four-legged beings, send this creature what he seeks. Banish the spell and his hold to me, as I will it so mote it be."

I tied the trio of ribbons around my first familiar and blew the herb from the charm Fiona gave me (witchbane root, representing the god of thunder) and blew it into the air.

I prayed like mad that it would work.

At first, nothing happened, and Thor looked a little cranky that I had interrupted his nap for this nonsense.

But then, right before my eyes, his skin stretched and popped, his muscles bulged, his fur darkened, his legs lengthened, and his entire frame shot into the air, and majestically—he morphed into a gorgeous black horse.

His body was shiny, his legs strong, and his mane kempt. He had just a streak of silver running the length of his head, but his eyes—his huge chocolate eyes—were filled with such love of a gentle soul that I wanted to cry.

Gingerly he approached me and lowered his head. I patted his nose and said, "You're welcome."

He galloped off into the forest. And I hoped, with his release, the others would find their peace.

"I feel like I'm forgetting something," Leo said to Gus.

I had just sat down in his office.

"Yeah, me too," said Gus.

Good. Fiona was right; the Chihuahua had been erased from their memories. I nudged the dog bed just far enough out of sight that I hoped Leo wouldn't notice it for a while.

"Should I come back?" I asked."No. You stay put. It'll come to me."

I just smiled as Gus walked out, scratching his head.

"What did you want to talk about?" I asked.

Leo rose and shut the door. He pulled a file from a basket on his desk. "Cole Tripp. That's the name of the guy we pulled from the lake. The ME was able to lift his prints and he was in the system."

I opened the folder to find a photograph of a scruffy man with small eyes that had seen their share of cruelty. His face had more lines than it should, judging from his date of birth, and his jaw was set to a deep scowl. If he were the attendant on duty at a gas station on a dark night, I would keep driving. The face I saw in the lake was the same one, but different too and not just because he was dead. It nagged at me.

Leo said, "Guy just got out of prison a week ago. Spent fourteen years in Joliet."

I glanced up. "For what?"

"Arson, drugs, manslaughter."

My eyes widened.

"He was operating a rolling meth lab and it blew up. Killed a woman in the car behind him."

"A rolling meth lab? Wow."

"It wasn't his first offense either. The guy had a record longer than my arm. Mostly drug related." Leo leaned back in his chair and said, "So, can you tell me why a man like that would be looking for you?"

My mind was a complete blank. Could I have been wrong? Was this man not connected to my father in any way? Or perhaps Dad was working on this guy's story?

That's when that voice came back to me. *I have the tapes.*

Geez, if there was some evidence my father possessed that connected this guy to more drug dealers, that would have certainly put his life at risk.

And mine if they suspected I had access to it. Thor was a pretty good source of protection, but something more powerful and portable might be in order now.

I looked up from the file and said, "Will you teach me how to shoot?"

"Shoot what?"

"You know, pistols, firearms, guns. I'm thinking of getting one and I want to learn how to use it properly."

"You did all right when you grabbed mine the night of the fire and shot into that keg."

I shrugged. "Beginner's luck. So will you?"

"No."

"Why not?"

"Because you're already dangerous. The town doesn't need you armed and dangerous."

Well, that was insulting.

Leo narrowed his eyes and leaned his face over the desk to stare at me. He was so close I could see the tiny scar on his cheek. He smelled like ginger and clove. "What are you not telling me?"

"Someone shot at me and Derek," I blurted out, and then the whole messy story poured from me in no particular chronological order.

He looked confused as I spoke. Then angry, then back to confused. When I finished I was pretty sure he was thinking Derek and I weren't the only ones who had dodged a bullet.

"I should have you arrested, you know that?" He stood up and shut the blinds. "Dammit, Stacy!"

"For what?"

"For what? Are you kidding me? Don't play dumb—you know what you did was completely reckless, irresponsible, and, and…"

"Icky?" I offered.

He ran his hand through his thick dark hair and sighed. "I was thinking more along the lines of obstruction of justice, trespassing, theft, but sure, let's go with icky."

"I only borrowed that tractor. I wasn't stealing it, and I had permission to be on Scoog's land." Which reminded me. "By the way, do you know how he died?"

"Don't change the subject."

I stood up. "Look, you can help me figure out what all of this has to do with my father's death and I will cooperate as best I can or I can just leave now and figure it out on my own. Your choice."

"Sit. Down. Please."

He took a deep breath, hit an intercom button, and asked Amy to bring him some aspirin.

"Parker keeps a bottle on his desk," I said, helpfully.

"I can't imagine why," Leo said.

I let that one slide as Amy bounced into the room with a bottle of water and two Advil. "Here you go." She waved at me as she scooted out the door.

"She's kind of cute." I lowered myself back into the chair.

Leo looked at me as if a second head had just sprouted from my neck. "She's about fifteen years old and Monique's cousin."

That reminded me. I grabbed a notebook from my bag and jotted down the messages that Derek's and Monique's ancestors had relayed to me. I flipped the page and slapped the book on Leo's desk.

"Are you going to be nice to me?" I asked.

"Are you going to keep me informed on your investigation and any tricks you may have up your sleeve?"

I cocked an eyebrow. "As I recall, that was a source of contention between us."

"You know what I mean."

"Sure."

He reached for the file on Cole Tripp and placed it on top of some other paperwork. "As for Scoog, no results yet, but there were no visible wounds. Most likely the guy just had a heart attack."

Dead men tell no tales. Maybe he died of natural causes, but there was nothing natural about the way he was trying to communicate with me.

"What about Liberty?"

"The bird? We found a place a few hours north that functions as a sanctuary. She's at the vet. She'll be transported tomorrow."

That made me a little sad for some reason. I hoped she would find another mate. Maybe I could drag Derek to the vet to say good-bye.

"As for our floater, he was hit over the head before his body was dumped in the lake."

"Did you find a car?" I jotted down notes.

Leo shook his head. "Not yet. The head injury is off the record, by the way. Whatever it was that he got hit with was unusually shaped, so we're keeping that under wraps for the time being."

"Okay." I looked up from my notes and saw Leo punching the keys on his computer.

He wrinkled his brow.

"What?"
"I just pulled up your dad's accident report."
"And?"
"There was no driver in the other vehicle."

Chapter 25

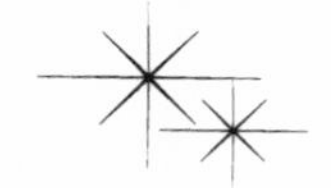

Leo explained that after the crash, whoever was driving the truck that hit my father had bailed. This was a point that I didn't remember or didn't pay attention to in my young, grief-stricken state.

Apparently the truck was registered to a company that hauled goods all over the US, Canada, and Mexico.

"The manager reported it stolen not long after the crash, so it had to be lifted somewhere nearby," Leo said.

Which made sense, although it offered little comfort.

I was still standing at another dead end.

Before I left, Leo told me he was heading back out to Scoog's place to do a sweep around Dad's car for bullet casings and to see why someone wouldn't want me inspecting it. He also said he would check to see if the truck had been towed there.

"If nothing else, I can get a warrant to access Scoog's ledgers. From what I understand, there is no next of kin who would object to it."

He handed me a copy of the accident report, and I told him I'd keep in touch. Then he grabbed my arm and twirled me into his chest. His gun pressed into my thigh.

At least I think it was his gun.

"I know this is personal for you, Stacy." He held my eyes and a flashback of the days he used to call me kitten swept through my mind. "But please be smart about this. You have trouble, you come to me. And here..." His arm slipped from mine and he reached into his desk. Tossed me a can of pepper spray. "It doesn't have the octane you were looking for, but it also won't upset your boyfriend. I suspect he wouldn't be too happy if you spent time with me at the shooting range."

It was three o'clock then. I picked up Thor and checked in with work. Derek had already written the piece on Cole Tripp, but I was able to fill in a few gaps with the information Leo had presented me.

I popped into Parker's office as he was piecing together tomorrow's edition.

"Derek took a beautiful picture of that collie you found." His long fingers hovered over the mouse, moving images and text to align them just right.

"She is a cutie," I said. "Parker, did you know the driver who hit my dad wasn't found at the scene?"

"Uh-huh." The monitor was huge and I could see he was having trouble fitting the Black Opal ad next to the classifieds.

"Don't you think that's a bit odd?"

Parker shrugged and a piece of dried skin flaked off from his sunburn. "Not if he was drunk. Or high."

"You think that's what happened, don't you?"

Parker looked at me. "Who else would steal a big rig?"

Good point.

"I just wish I had his files," I mumbled.

"What's that you said?" He was still engrossed in his computer screen.

I sighed, told him it was nothing, and walked out, closing the door behind me.

When I turned around, I smacked head-on into Iris.

She had a sheepish grin on her face.

"Were you eavesdropping?"

She shrugged. "I'm a gossip columnist." She said it without a trace of shame in her voice.

I laughed, told her I had to run, and made my way to the parking lot.

Iris followed me. "Stacy, wait!"

I had my keys in my hand as I turned around. Thor was waiting for me next to the car. "What's up?"

"What files were you talking about?"

"Oh." I waved my hand. "It's nothing. Just what my dad was working on before he passed."

Iris cocked her head, wagged a finger at me. "You know. I just may be able to help you out, kiddo."

I drove Iris to her small house on Crescent Moon Drive listening to her babble about treasure hunting.

"I hit 'em all, but the best one is the Spring Clean at the community center. I once bought a teapot there with only one chip in it."

"Only one? Wow."

She was talking about garage sales. Apparently the earlier you got to one the better the deals, and it was best to carry pictures of your collections to make sure that you didn't purchase a duplicate. And to wear comfortable shoes.

I had never been inside Iris's house before and I must say it was incredibly clean, with the lingering scent of pine oil and orange Pledge. It was also a little creepy.

She had about twenty thousand PEZ dispensers, all shapes and sizes, including the very rare (according to her) Daffy Duck on a black stand. She had neatly organized them in curio cabinets according to color.

There were also shelves and shelves of salt and pepper shakers lining every wall. I wasn't sure what inspired a person to purchase a set of salt and pepper shakers in the form of a dog whizzing on a fire hydrant, but hey, we all have our obsessions.

Even Thor looked utterly amazed.

Iris flipped on a light and opened a door. "Electronics and things are in the basement."

My jaw dropped as I descended the stairs. Stacks of Atari gaming systems, eight-track players, cassette tapes, VHS and beta boxes, turntables, and computers that dated back to Plato teetered against the walls.

I stood there, gobsmacked, as Iris filtered through her collections.

"Got it!" she said after just ten minutes of searching. She handed me a round, black nylon bag.

Inside were computer disks. One—the last one—was labeled SJ in blue ink.

My throat closed up for a moment. "Where did you get this?" I finally asked.

Iris explained that the bed-and-breakfast association put on a yearly sale to raise funds for advertising dollars.

"I'm sure your grandmother didn't realize what it was." She glanced around the room. "Heck, I didn't even know until I logged it."

I hugged Iris and told her I'd buy her a salt and pepper shaker set the next time I was at a flea market.

As Thor and I walked out, I received a text from Tony. *Cin's not answering her phone. Can you check on her?*

I drove to Cinnamon's house, all the while itching to crack into the CD case. If I had my laptop with me, I would have.

Cinnamon didn't answer the door right away. I peeked through the window and saw that she was getting up off the couch.

She answered the door in a tank top and shorts. "Hey, Cousin."

"Hey, you okay?"

"Of course, just got up from a nap. Why?" She left the door open and walked toward the kitchen, her long dark waves bouncing off her back.

Thor and I followed. "Tony asked me to check on you."

She poured herself a glass of orange juice and drank it in one gulp. "That man worries too much. I think I caught a bug, that's all." She smiled. "What's up? Anything new?"

I told her about Cole Tripp, the driver from Dad's accident (or lack thereof), my conversation with Leo, and the CDs.

She set her glass on the counter with force, splashed water on her face, and said, "CDs first, then we shoot."

I sat back in the computer chair a few minutes later and shook my head. "I can't believe it."

"Me neither," said Cin.

Every disk was blank. There was a code written on the back of one of them—GGGH225, but that didn't ring a bell. I wanted to pull my hair out and holler until I was hoarse.

Cinnamon tapped my knee. "Come on. I know something that'll cheer you up. Almost as good as sex."

"Really?"

I watched my cousin as she pulled a large duffel bag out from beneath the bed and unzipped it. The woman had an arsenal almost as impressive as Iris's PEZ collection. There were holsters for every body part, six-shooters, semiautomatic pistols, revolvers, and more.

If there was one thing my uncle Deck taught his daughter, it was how to handle a weapon. A police officer himself, he wanted to ensure that Cin would always be able to protect herself. My mother hated guns so I was never allowed to participate in these sessions.

Cin's personal shooting gallery was behind Tony's garage. We drove there with her collection.

Thor plopped down in the shade as Cinnamon set up the target. I could hear the sound of power tools filtering from the shop as I waited.

When she was done, a life-sized portrait of Monique Fontaine stared at me.

I frowned.

She poked me and said, "Come on, it's funny. Besides"—she handed me a pair of goggles and earmuffs, then put some on herself—"it helps me deal with my anger toward her, and this way, I don't physically act on it."

I raised my eyebrows.

"Okay, I don't act on it as often." She loaded a magazine into a semiautomatic and shot Monique's cowboy hat off.

Fair enough. I guess if a woman had lied to the town about my husband having an affair, which prompted me to divorce him, I'd want to shoot her too.

"I'll turn it around to Joe Schmo and then you try."

She holstered the gun and I stared at it as she jogged toward the cutout.

I wasn't a fan of guns, which made me nervous to hold one. Maybe this was a mistake. Maybe Leo was right.

But then I decided that if I was going to be shot at, I may as well learn to shoot back.

Cinnamon turned the plywood around to reveal the silhouette of a man with white rings covering his body. When she was finished, she returned to my side.

"You ready?"

"Do you have anything smaller?" I asked.

"Sure." She fumbled around in her bag. "This is a .38 special revolver. It's not loaded. Go ahead and feel it out."

It was lighter than I thought it would be. The barrel was short, the grip was made of black rubber, and it felt comfortable in my small hands.

"Okay, lesson one." Cinnamon turned toward me. "Safety first. Assume that all guns are always loaded."

I nodded.

"Never point"—Cin lifted her weapon and aimed it at the target—"at anything you are not willing to destroy. Don't put your finger on the trigger until you have your sites on your target." She cupped the gun with both hands. "And finally, understand what will happen when you pull it." She set her feet shoulder width apart, her right leg back slightly, bent her knees a bit, and fired into Joe Schmo's crotch.

"Nice aim."

"Thanks."

A few doors down, someone lit a grill for a cook-out.

Cinnamon taught me a few more lessons along with different stances for different situations plus the proper way to holster, draw, and hold the weapon. She explained the paperwork I needed to register with the state and that it might take awhile to get approved. We practiced shooting for about an hour. After that, I prodded her for information on the Hell Hounds.

"I don't know a lot about them. They've played for me a few times over the years."

"Ever heard of any of them getting into trouble? Anyone talk about them around town?"

Cin thought for a moment as she inspected each weapon to make sure it was unloaded. "You know, since you mention it, Huck always called them 'those damn hippies.'" She shrugged. "I just figured it was because they had long hair and smoked weed or something."

Mr. Huckleberry owned the building that housed my cousin's bar.

I helped Cin pack up and she explained the dynamics of the band. Brian was the lead singer. The guy who looked perpetually stoned was a friend from high school, and the Perrier drinker with the short hair was Brian's neighbor. The woman with the skull tattoo was Becky, a new addition. Apparently there were perks to dating a musician.

"You know how it goes. They play together today, but different members have come and gone over the years. It's really Brian's band." She zipped up her duffel bag and said, "Why are you asking me all this anyway?"

I glanced at Thor, who was trying to catch a bee. "I just got a weird vibe from him."

"Really? Brian? I always thought he was sweet."

I shifted my gaze from Thor to my cousin. The sun was at her back and the effect of the light through the trees gave the image of a golden hue all around her body.

"But I could be wrong," Cin said.

She hoisted the bag across her back and walked toward the car. I called for Thor and we followed her.

I watched her walk and noticed that the luminosity never left her. It moved with her body, hovered all around her.

That's when I knew.

Chapter 26

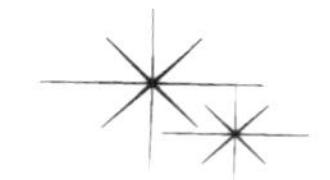

"Oh my God, you're pregnant!" I said.

She dropped the bag and rushed forward. Clamped a hand over my mouth. "Be quiet! I'm not pregnant." She shook her head.

I bobbed mine up and down and said, "Yes you are." Except her hand was so tight over my pie hole it sounded more like, *Yeth u arf.*

Cinnamon sighed and dropped her hand. "Okay, maybe. I'm a little late, but I haven't taken a test yet."

"Why not?"

"Well, for starters, I never get any alone time except at the bar and I don't want Tony to know just yet."

"Again, why not? He'd be thrilled."

Tony was the kind of man who would rather spend time with his wife than take a night out with the boys. He adored my cousin and bragged about her constantly. Who could blame him? Cin was smart, sexy, a hard worker, and a ton of fun.

"Because I need a little time to think of a good reason why I should keep the bar." Cin started pacing. "I mean, geez, what am I going to do? Bake cookies like my mother?"

Mama Angelica's bakery was legendary in these parts.

"You think he'd ask you to do that?"

"I don't know." She started talking with her hands—an indicator that she was anxious about this. "He's a worrier. I can't think of too many husbands who would be thrilled with the idea of his wife slinging drinks at obnoxious drunks with a sixth-month belly bump."

I caught her hand and said, "First off, Tony isn't like most husbands. Second, there's no sense in worrying just yet. Why don't I come by the bar tonight and take the test with you?"

She looked somewhat relieved and agreed to the arrangement as long as I picked up the tests the next town over.

We packed up the car and I dropped her off.

She leaned into the window and said, "Be there before eight. Band starts at nine." She started away, but I saw she had left the .38 on the floor of the car tucked inside an ankle holster.

"Cin. You forgot one."

She turned and said, "If there are two things I know about you, Cuz, it's that you wouldn't use that thing unless you absolutely had to. The other is that you may absolutely have to."

I watched her walk into the house, hoping she was wrong.

Leo called on my way to the cottage.

"We did a sweep of your dad's car and it's clean. No cut wires, nothing out of the ordinary with the engine or brakes. We also didn't find any shell casings."

"So the shooter got there first."

"No bullet holes either. There could be another explanation for what happened."

"Such as?"

"We found BBs."

"Come again?"

"BBs. We think maybe it was kids screwing around. They've been known to aim at abandoned cars before."

"Geez, it's not enough that they torture the Shelby goats, now they're taking shots at random people?"

Because they sure sounded like real bullets.

"I'm not saying I won't keep looking into it, but that's the view from out here. We did find the truck. Dusted it for prints, but I suspect they'll belong to a lot of different people."

I disconnected with him and immediately my phone rang again. It was Derek. "Are you forgetting something?"

Crap. I was his ride. "Be right there."

Derek hobbled over to the car and jumped in the passenger seat. He was sweating a lot for someone who just exited an air-conditioned building. He searched through his bag, pulled out a pen, and stuck it down the boot. "Man, this thing itches!"

A dog barked in the distance and Thor answered.

I felt sorry for Derek. The summer I broke my leg playing kick-ball I had to wear that stinky cast for six weeks. It was hot, itchy, and not waterproof.

"Can't you take it off?"

"Yeah, I did last night."

He twisted the air vent in the car to aim it at his face. Then he reached for a magazine as I pulled the car out of the parking lot.

"Do you need a ride tomorrow?" I asked when we got to his apartment.

"Nah, I think I can manage. I wasn't sure if I was going to pop a pain pill, but it doesn't feel too bad anymore."

He folded up the magazine and I saw it was a catalog for the spy store. I was about to tease him about it when I spotted something on the back cover.

"Derek, can I see that for a minute?"

"Sure." Thor whinnied in the backseat. "Hang on, buddy, almost home."

A closer look confirmed my initial assessment. But I wasn't positive until I held the watch from the lake up to the ad. Some of the features looked an awful lot like the wristwatch on the back of the spy catalog. The caption read, *Voice-activated digital audio recorder. Capture meeting minutes, business agreements, or interviews discreetly and effectively.*

Could this be the tapes?

"Derek, where is the spy store?"

"It's in Dubuque. On Thirteenth Street."

Twenty minutes away.

"Get back in the car."

"What, nooooo. Come on, I'm hungryyyyy," he whined, and Thor thought that was his cue to chime in.

The dog lifted his head and howled.

"Stop that! Both of you. I'll stop at Aztec Tacos, okay?"

That seemed to shut them both up.

We found a spot right out front of the spy store. Thor devoured a king burrito while I filled Derek in on the story. He admired the watch as I spoke.

"So hopefully there's a chance that the recordings are still on here. Maybe that's what the caller meant. Not actual cassette or video tapes but taped recordings."

Derek cocked an eyebrow at me. "And you think the same stiff they pulled from the lake is the one who called you."

"I'm almost positive."

"Well," Derek said and sipped his soda, "if anyone can retrieve whatever data is on here, it's Sydney."

As he finished off his taco, I thought of a way to bring up the message I was supposed to relay to him from the great-aunt I met at the cemetery. What did she say the name of her sister was? Maybel. That was it.

The way I saw it, this might be my first break and I wasn't about to piss off the spirits.

"Hey, by the way, someone named Maybel called for you."

"Maybel?" He chewed slowly, reached for more hot sauce, and said, "I don't know a Maybel."

Could I have gotten it wrong or did I now have to worry about ghosts lying to me?

"She said she was your grandmother."

Derek widened his eyes briefly and then said, "My grandmother's name is Maybelline. And she's been in a convent for five years. Doesn't phone home too much."

He was staring me down.

I bluffed as best I could. "Well, she wants you to go back to law school."

"You sure it wasn't my mother who called?"

"Could have been."

He crumpled up his taco wrappers and tossed them into the bag. "That woman never gives up, I swear. You know why I came all the way out here after college instead of staying back east or going south where my koo-koo auntie is?"

"It was the only place hiring?"

"Well, there was that, but mostly to get away from the elite attitude that success is defined by a million-dollar house and a Mercedes." He shrugged. "I like my job. I like it here. It's quiet and friendly, and most days no one's trying to shoot me."

"Well, don't tell her I told you. She asked me to be subtle."

Derek snorted. "You, subtle? Ha!" He tossed out the trash and called to Thor. "Sydney loves dogs. He thinks they're the perfect place to plant a spy camera or a bug." He held the door open and we all walked in.

Sydney looked like a spy camera. Or a bug. He had huge eyes magnified by Coke-bottle glasses that his tiny nose struggled to support. There was one streak of dark hair, combed in all different directions as if he couldn't settle on just one, and his vest had more pockets than a big-game hunter's.

"Well, hello there." He whipped off his glasses and made googly eyes at me.

Apparently Sydney also fancied himself a ladies' man. Although unwanted advances didn't really bother me much.

"Whoa, easy, fella. Good dog, good boy." Sydney jumped back, trembling near a shelf of teddy bear cameras. "I was just being friendly."

Thor was standing at full height, paws on Sydney's counter. He growled softly once and then flared his teeth simply for showmanship.

"Thor, that's enough," I said.

"Fine-looking dog you have there, miss."

I smiled as Derek took control of the conversation.

"Hey, Syd, we have an older model audio recorder here. Thing was submerged in water. You think you could work your magic?"

That reminded me, I had to get back for my training. I checked the time. Around this time, Birdie and the aunts were likely serving refreshments, which meant I had about an hour.

Sydney attached some sort of scope on the end of his glasses so now he looked like a bug from outer space.

He squinted at the watch and said, "Maybe. Usually if there's too much water damage this little dot right here turns red." He showed us a black dot. Then he took off the extra eyewear. "Got a few cases ahead of yours, but I should be able to get back to you next week."

"Next week? Can't you fit it in a bit sooner? I'll pay extra," I pleaded.

Thor was inspecting a pair of doggie goggles with a built-in camera. He cocked his head toward Sydney and waited for a response.

Derek said, "She's Lolly's great-niece."

Sydney looked a bit mortified at that. He took a step back. "Oh. Okay, tell you what, little lady, since my best customer is your friend here and, um, Lolly is your relation, I'll move you up on the list. I should have something by tomorrow. How's that?"

"Thank you, Sydney."

Derek slapped the doggie goggles along with a bandana on the counter for Thor and I paid for all the purchases, including Derek's new spyglasses.

Thor stood a little taller as Derek slipped the goggles over his ears. If he had a spiked collar to complete the ensemble, the dog would have looked like a Hell's Angel.

"Thor, say thank you to Uncle Derek."

Derek was adjusting the bandana around Thor's neck. He stuck his hand in the air and Thor met it with a high five.

We made a quick stop at the drugstore the next block up, where I ran in and bought two pregnancy tests and shoved them in my bag. I dropped Derek off at his apartment and headed toward the cottage. I changed quickly into jean shorts and a one-shoulder top, applied some fresh makeup, and brushed out my hair, partly to be ready to head to the Black Opal and partly so Fiona wouldn't nag about my appearance.

I was ready then. Ready to become the woman I was born to be.

Chapter 27

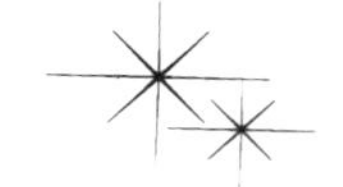

"Dogs never bite me. Just humans."
—Marilyn Monroe

I decided to leave Thor in the yard with a fresh bowl of water and a chewy bone. It had cooled down considerably and he enjoyed bird watching as much as they enjoyed riding him like a hippo.

The back door was unlocked so I let myself in and called to Birdie. No answer, but the door to the back stairs creaked open, inviting me in like a scene from a horror movie that makes you yell at the screen and want to shake the stupid girl who's about to walk into an ambush.

Naturally, I passed through the threshold.

The stairs were dark, but I saw Lolly's wedding dress hanging at the top on a coat rack and made a mental note to meet with the metal sculptor. I wondered if the aunts and Birdie knew that Jack's cousin was living just outside of town. I hoped I could find some answers for her. Some peace.

I ducked my head into each of their rooms and found only Keesha, resting comfortably. I scratched her head and said, "See you tomorrow. Vet appointment. Don't be late."

I approached the hidden lair.

I spent many years in this house, but it wasn't until a few months ago that Fiona led me to a hidden room behind the gilded gold painting of the Celtic goddess Danu. In her hand, she held an intricately carved chalice and on the chalice was a sparkling ruby. I pressed the ruby as Fiona had done and Danu's eyes met mine with approval. I thought she winked at me, but I couldn't be sure.

The frame shook violently and then swung wide, opening to the mouth of the passageway. I followed it as far as I could. The brick wall came at me fast and I stopped, but not before I smacked it with my nose.

"Ouch."

My eyes squeezed shut, I took three deep breaths and imagined a doorway to replace the brick. The brick buckled and pulsed, finally rippling into a white-framed door tall enough to walk through.

"Hey," I said to Birdie. "I made it bigger this time."

"Very good, Anastasia."

The room was still anchored by the massive round table. It was made of oak and carved with Celtic symbols such as triquetras, trees-of-life, and triskeles, as well as gods and goddesses, battle scenes, and other images of Ireland.

Lolly was setting up a screen at the far side of the room and Fiona was sifting through the wardrobe. She grabbed a light sweater and sat at one of the red velvet chairs.

Something was wrong here. No one was wearing a ritual cape. There were no herbs, crystals, athames.

This was not what a training session with these witches usually looked like.

"Why isn't anyone dressed?"

Lolly looked at me with raised eyebrows. She had a highball in her hand and she was wearing a peach cocktail dress with halter straps that looked like it came from Marilyn Monroe's closet.

"You know what I mean," I said.

Birdie sat down next to Fiona and said, "Well, dear, your official training was not to begin until the summer solstice."

"So?"

"So we weren't prepared," Fiona said. There was a bowl of popcorn on the table and she offered it to me. I declined.

"But the solstice is Friday. That's not far off. Surely you must be able to teach me something that would be more beneficial than watching a movie."

Birdie reached for the popcorn and said, "Sit down, Anastasia. You might learn something."

So I sat. Lolly flipped the light switch and Fiona turned on the projector.

The film was shaky, as if it had been shot long ago with poor equipment. It opened with a view of the rich Irish hillside. Then a female voice that I recognized as Maegan's, my great-grandmother, began to speak. She described Ireland and her many secrets, showing scenes of such iconic landmarks as the Hill of Tara—the ancient seat of power. One hundred and forty-two kings were said to have reigned there and it was believed to have been a realm into the otherworld where the gods resided. It went on to explain how Woodhenge, similar to England's Stonehenge, was constructed around the Hill and how it was used for inauguration ceremonies.

The next shot was of the Stone of Destiny, thought to have been brought to the Hill of Tara by the Tuatha Dé Danann, the red-haired, fair-skinned magical people of the goddess Danu. Legend has it that the stone would roar when touched by the rightful king of the land. Next, Maegan talked about the three other treasures brought to the island by the Danann: Dagda's Cauldron, from which none left hungry; Spear of Lugh, which would secure victory for the warrior who held it; and the Sword of Light of Núada, from which none could escape once drawn.

Maegan said, "Beneath her bosom, Tara holds great secrets you are beholden to protect at all costs."

A half an hour had passed at that time and I was growing impatient. How was this supposed to help me catch a killer?

I shut off the projector and asked Birdie just that. Lolly, seated closest to the lights, got up and turned them on.

My grandmother tilted her head and said, "That's not what you requested. You asked us to teach you how to be the Seeker of Justice. This is your legacy, child, this is your destiny. This is what you must embrace if you are to retrieve your mother come Samhain."

My mother, faced with a difficult choice to protect me, committed a high crime, according to some council that my family was involved with back in Ireland. It was agreed that I would speak on her behalf and try to bring her home. But her hearing wasn't until October 31, four months down the road. There was nothing I could do for her now. Right now, my focus was on finding out what happened to my father.

I said all this to Birdie and she stood to address me.

"Listen to me. Do not tread into dark waters when we are so close to having your mother back. This thing can wait. I cannot have you hurting yourself or damaging everything we have accomplished. The Council was pleased with your performance on protecting the page of Ballymote." She was referring to a quest she sent me on a few months ago. "It was the only reason they agreed to an early hearing." She grasped my shoulders, then dropped her hands as if she had been burned.

She studied me for a moment, her eyes dancing up and down my body. "What has happened to your heart?"

"What? Nothing has happened to my heart. It's right where I left it."

She began sniffing me like Thor does when I've been around another dog. She grabbed my hands and held them up to the light.

"What have you been doing?"

"Birdie, I really don't know what you're talking about." Because I didn't.

She grabbed my satchel from near the door and sifted through it.

"Hey! Stop that!"

She pulled Cinnamon's gun out of the bag and I ducked. "Be careful with that! Put it back."

"What is this?" she demanded.

"A gun. Cinnamon gave it to me," I said, throwing my cousin under the bus.

"This is not the way we do things."

"Are you kidding me? Lolly strapped me up with enough hardware on that 'mission' you sent me on to take down a terrorist cell."

"That was different."

"How?"

Fiona said, "Well, dear, we knew you were heading into danger. We needed you protected." She took off her sweater. "And we didn't know the boots were loaded."

Lolly said, "That's why I gave you the knife." Then she chewed on an ice cube.

"The difference," Birdie said in a tone reserved for when she wanted to emphasize she was older and wiser than me, "is that you were forced into a situation that put you in harm's way. You were being hunted." She held up the gun. "But this tells me that you are the one who is hunting."

She put the gun in the bag and set it on the floor next to the chair between us.

I stared at it for a beat, put my hands on the back of the chair. She was wrong; she was wrong about this one. Every nerve in my body told me so. She couldn't see past her worry about my mother.

I raised my voice, held it firm. "I am seeking justice."

"You are seeking revenge!" Her fury vibrated the room.

"And what if I am, Grandmother, so what? Don't we abide by Celtic law?" I flashed my right hand toward the blank screen and it snapped and twirled up into itself.

Birdie yelled a Celtic triad at me. "Three things without which the protection of the Mighty Ones cannot be: forgiving an enemy and a wrong done; wisdom in judgment and act; cleaving to what is just, come what may."

Behind me, a frame leaped off the wall and crashed to the floor.

I fired back. "Three things only a fool calls imprudent: to seek knowledge, come what will; to give alms openly; and to endure for truth and justice without fear of what may come."

The projector spun off the table and slammed onto the floor.

"Why do you think the tiger has appeared?"

"To warn me of danger."

"Wrong!" She slammed her hands down on the table. Behind her, the door cracked and flew off its hinges. "To warn you not to make the same mistakes your mother did."

I tightened my grip on the chair. "The difference is"—I leaned forward—"I won't get caught!"

The chair shook in my grip and shattered into a heap of dust and debris.

Birdie stared at the broken pieces, flicked her eyes to her sisters. Finally she looked at me.

"If you pursue this, you do so without me."

I picked up my bag, stepped over the pile, and stared her down.

"I wouldn't have it any other way."

Chapter 28

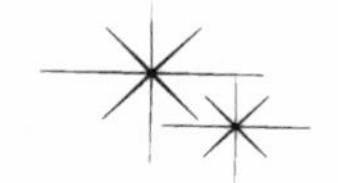

I was shaking as I stormed out of the house, but I couldn't let the scene with Birdie affect what I had to do.

This was my mission, my responsibility to my father to find out why he was killed.

And to bring down whoever was behind it.

I had plenty of time before I was supposed to meet Cinnamon, so I went back to the cottage, grabbed the mail, and tucked the gun into my underwear drawer. I cranked the air on for Thor and removed his spy goggles and bandana. He settled into the couch while I reached for the CD case that Iris had given me.

One by one, I checked the disks again, even consulted the Blessed Book (my family's magical grimoire) for an electronic retrieval spell, but came up short.

I flipped through the mail. Bills, advertisements, more bills.

But something clicked into place.

I snatched the last CD off my desk and looked at the code on the back again.

GGGH225.

GGGH—Geraghty Girls' Guesthouse.

The address of the cottage was 225 before they purchased the lot and incorporated it into their business. Long before I moved in. My dad would have known that.

Did he wipe the disks after he printed out the information and bury the files here on the property? Hide them inside the house?

Why would he do that?

Unless…he knew he was in danger and it was his insurance policy.

I got busy tearing the place apart, searching under, up, over, and inside every nook and cranny I could find. I looked under drawers, inside cabinets, closets, the crawl space, the tiny attic nook, even pulled out the refrigerator and the washer and dryer.

An hour later, I was covered in dirt, grease, cobwebs, and grime and had nothing whatsoever to show for it.

"Agh!"

Thor trotted over to me and sat down. He cocked his head.

I reached out to pet him and said, "Sorry, buddy. Didn't mean to scare you." I picked up the CD and slumped into a chair, staring at it as if the answer would magically appear.

My date with Cin was fast approaching and I needed a shower. Just before I got up to do that, Thor nudged the hand holding the CD.

"That's not a chew toy, mister."

He nudged again, sniffed it thoroughly. Then he sauntered over to the half wall between the living room and the kitchen and slapped it.

I stood up, looked at the CD, and then looked at Thor. "You sure?"

He grumbled at me and slapped the wall again, chipping some paint.

I examined every inch of the wall, knocking up and down it. There were no outlets that I could find. No heating ducts or vents. I knocked all around the space and it seemed hollow.

Chance had bought me a toolbox for the house about a month ago. I ran to the back closet and searched through it. The hammer didn't seem efficient enough for what I was about to do. But I remembered he had left a sledgehammer by the back door from when he pounded in the posts for Thor's dog house.

I grabbed it, then said a silent prayer that there was no plumbing, electrical, or otherwise necessary equipment for modern-day comforts hidden behind the wall.

I arched the sledgehammer back and took a mighty swing at the sucker.

"You're late," Cinnamon said.

"Fifteen minutes. That's nothing."

"Get in here."

She yanked me into her office, shut and locked the door.

"Why do you look like you got into a fight with the Pillsbury Doughboy?"

"I toweled off." I'd had no time for a shower after I knocked the wall down.

She bit her nail. "Did you bring it?"

"Yep. Got one for each of us." I shook the boxes.

"You go first."

This whole *take the test with me idea* was so girly that I couldn't help but feel all soft and mushy. My cousin was not the girly-girl type and sometimes I wished we had more bonding experiences that didn't involve firearms or flamethrowers.

"Wipe that stupid grin off your face."

Yeah, that was more like her. "Fine. Be right back."

I took the test, enjoying the scent of citrus from the restroom air freshener, then washed up and used the toiletries in her private bathroom to make myself look less like the new guy on a construction crew. Except now I looked like the only albino cast member on *The Jersey Shore*. I think I overdid it with the hair spray.

I slipped out and waited for Cinnamon to take her turn. A minute later, the sink was running. Then Cin stepped out and we waited. She handed me a timer. I set the timer according to the directions on the package and shoved both empty packages back into my bag.

Cin paced as I filled her in on what I found.

"You didn't have a chance to read any of it yet?"

"Not yet. Chance is meeting me, so the minute he gets here, I'll probably head home."

Cin gave me a grave look.

"You want me to stay?"

"No, you don't have to." But the answer was really *yes*.

Since the folder had been tucked away for all this time, I guess it couldn't hurt to wait one more day.

The timer dinged a few minutes later and Cinnamon sucked in her breath.

"You want me to check?" I asked.

"I'll do it."

I stood up and followed her into the bathroom.

Cinnamon gasped and said, "They're both positive!"

"What?" I grabbed the sticks from her hand and read them. I glared at her.

She chuckled. "You should have seen your face."

I hugged her. "Congratulations, Mama."

She sighed and said, "Ready or not."

"You're going to be great at it."

Someone knocked on the door. "The band's all set up. They went to grab a quick bite."

"Thanks," said Cinnamon. We walked out and I asked if she needed me to do anything. She declined and got busy inspecting the bar to make sure it was fully stocked for the evening.

I ordered a glass of wine from the young bartender and sat down just as Monique Fontaine sashayed through the door wearing a mesh tube top and leopard skirt. I downed half the glass of wine in an effort to gain some courage for what I could only assume was going to be an awkward conversation.

How was I going to relay to Monique that her great-great-grandmother was proud of her?

"Hey, Monique," I said as she walked up to the bar.

She took one look at me and said, "Hey, Snooki."

I couldn't really blame her for that one. I patted my hair down and tried again. "Not working tonight?"

She plopped her boobs on the bar and ordered a white zinfandel. "No, Stacy, I am working." She swept her arms around her and said, "This is all done with smoke and mirrors."

Kinda wished I brought the gun at that point.

She fluffed her hair and said, "Hello? I'm closed on Mondays, remember?"

Thor ambled over and sprawled at my feet.

"Jesus Christ, does this beast have to escort you everywhere?" She smoothed out her skirt and said, "He's getting dog slobber all over my Manolos."

Sometimes you just have to hug it out. I downed the rest of my wine, tossed my arms around Monique, and said, "I'm proud of you."

She pushed me into the next bar stool and said, "What the hell is wrong with you? Are you high?" To the bartender she said, "Harry, cancel the zin. I'll take a shot of tequila and a can of bug repellent."

Cinnamon was walking by, carrying a few glasses. "Monique, you are a can of bug repellent."

Monique shook her head. "I don't know why I come here."

Cin was bent over a cooler. "Neither do I."

This was not the way I hoped it would work out.

I paid for Monique's shot, grabbed her hand, and pulled her aside.

"Easy, easy, these are five-inch heels!" she squeaked.

I spun her toward the wall and said, "Okay, look. I know you don't like me or my family very much—"

"Your cousin is the anti-Christ."

"Whatever, just listen to me. I, I…"

Monique stuck her chin out. "What?"

The truth was probably not the best path. What came out sounded like one really long word. "I-had-a-dream-about-a-woman-in-a-flapper-dress-that-looked-like-you-and-she-wanted-me-to-tell-you-she's-proud-of-her-great-great-granddaughter."

Whew! Glad that was over.

Monique's eyes widened and she paused for a very long time. Then she laughed so hard, spittle landed on my face.

"You're a nut, you know that? Give me what you're smoking." She cackled all the way back to the bar, and I was sure before the evening was over everyone would have heard the story.

I liked her great-great-grandmother much better.

Then I thought, *Wait a minute, if she was as mean as Monique, I bet that bitch set me up.*

Couldn't even trust the dead.

Chapter 29

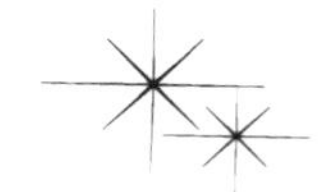

"A door is what a dog is perpetually
on the wrong side of."

—Ogden Nash

The band took the stage half an hour later. Becky sang the first song, a Joan Jett number. She was older than I thought, but I guess it's hard to assess someone's age by staring at the back of her head. She was shaking an ornamented tambourine against her hips. Brian was wailing on the guitar, while the spiky-haired guy, Sebastian, played a yellow bass. In the back, gearing up for a drum solo, was Rob, the one who dressed like an accountant.

The pulse in the room was electric, but I wasn't feeling any magic coming my way. I couldn't conjure up the image from the other day that had sparked from Brian. Maybe it leaped to me in the first place because I had touched him. Or maybe it was a mixed signal. Perhaps the energy of the music streaming off the stage that night collided with the energy from Cole Tripp's spirit leaving his body. He was killed—or at least sunk—close to where the band played.

I sipped my wine and applauded when the set ended. The band announced a short break and they all approached the bar for a round of refreshments.

Brian said, "How'd we do?"

"Fantastic," I said.

Becky was sucking down a glass of water on the other side of Brian.

"That's a gorgeous instrument," I told her, nodding to the tambourine.

"Thanks," she said.

Brain said, "I had it made special for her. Show her, Becks," Brain said.

She held it up, jiggled it a bit. There was a raven in the center, set between two crossed guitars. In rounded letters below it the word *Nevermore* was spelled out, save for a few letters.

"Are you a Poe fan?" I asked.

She nodded, breathing a bit heavy from the dancing, and sipped more water. "Unfortunately, the letters keep falling off." She smiled at me and I saw something familiar in her eyes before she excused herself and made her way to the bathroom.

Rob came up behind me and said, "Pretty good crowd for a Monday." He was wearing one of those super watches that told time in twenty-six countries.

I scanned the crowd. "Yep, not bad."

Someone bumped him from behind and his Heineken sloshed all over me.

"Oh, I'm so sorry." He reached for some napkins and patted down my arm.

When he did, a piercing pain blinded me for a moment and the vision came again of the man sinking to his watery grave.

I yanked my arm away. "It's okay. I'll just wash up in the bathroom." I backed away, a shaky smile on my face. "If I don't get in line now, I'll miss the next set!"

I hurried toward the ladies' room and smacked right into Becky.

"Sor—"

I doubled over in pain as the same vision hit me.

Geez, were they all in on it or had my mind just gone around the bend?

"You okay?" Becky asked.

I nodded. "Cramps." I swung through the door.

I stared into the black lacquer mirror as I tried to pull myself together.

None of this was going well. It was all too much too fast and I wondered if I was up to the task. My visions seemed completely distorted. No one wanted to hear the messages the dead sent me to deliver. The audio tapes may very well have been destroyed in the water and I hadn't found Keesha's family.

Maybe Birdie was right. Maybe I wasn't supposed to focus on my father's murder right now. After all, if that were the right direction, wouldn't I have received some sort of sign?

I splashed cold water on my face and washed away the beer, feeling defeated and cheated, wondering why the hell my father couldn't send me his own messages.

"Where are you?" I asked.

In a wave of energy, the mirror misted over and the white tiger appeared. She was poised on a grassy hillside, so close I could almost touch her. She trotted over to a large stone. There was a sword protruding from its belly and the glossy tiger perched next to it.

My sword. The three muses sword Birdie had given me. The engraving shimmered and illuminated, sending the letters dancing across the mirror.

Follow your instincts. Trust in your power. Defend your honor.

The door squeaked open then and the image fizzled as Thor poked his head inside.

I steadied my resolve and said, "I'm okay, buddy. Probably time to hit the road, huh?"

He made a Scooby sound and pulled his head back as the door swung shut.

I turned back to the mirror and said to my reflection, "Game on."

Chance was leaning against the bar, enjoying the music when I emerged.

"Hey!" He pulled me close and sunk his lips into mine. "You taste good," he whispered and swung me into a slow rhythm to the tune of a ballad I didn't recognize.

After a few minutes he said, "Sorry I had to work late. I'll make it up to you, though."

"You bet you will," I said. "I have something very specific in mind too."

He smiled wickedly and said in a sultry tone, "I like the sound of that. Let's get out of here."

"Sure. Let me just say good-bye to Cinnamon."

I grabbed my bag and headed around the bar where Cinnamon was berating a customer. "You point that finger at me one more time and I will rip it off and use it as a swizzle stick."

"Hey, Cin, I'm going to take off. You okay?"

The customer she was talking to said, "I think she has an anger management problem."

"I think you have a shut-the-hell-up problem. Order a drink that isn't pink." She said to me, "Freaking Sea Breeze, do you believe this guy?"

And that's when I knew she'd be just fine. I told her I'd call tomorrow, wished the guy on the bar stool good luck, and headed out with Chance.

The night air was heavy, with the faintest hint of caramel corn drifting over from the candy store. I looked up, happy to see the stars out in full force. One of the perks of living in a small town was the lack of city lighting that drowned nature's luminosity.

Chance opened the back of the pickup so Thor could enjoy a friendly breeze on the short ride home. "Busy day tomorrow?"

"You could say that." I told him I had to take Keesha to the vet, pop over to the spy store to follow up on a lead, read over some files, and possibly interview a metal sculptor for a profile piece. I also filled him in on my meeting with Leo and his findings regarding the Junkyard Graveyard, Mr. Scoog, and Cole Tripp.

We discussed all that for a few minutes before we pulled into the driveway.

At the cottage, Chance jogged around to the passenger door to open it for me and then lowered the back gate for Thor. I fumbled for my key as the dog jumped down and chased a croaking frog.

"Hey, Stacy, I was thinking it might be nice to go away this weekend. Just you and me."

I shoved the key in the lock and twisted. Then I turned to him. "It sounds like paradise, but Friday is the summer solstice. It's a big deal to Birdie. However…" I snaked my arms around his waist and kissed his neck. "We could lock ourselves in the cottage Saturday and Sunday." I kissed the other side. "Order delivery." Then his chin. "Listen to some music." Then his lips. "Get busy getting dirty."

His breath increased with each word, each kiss tensed his muscles, and I could feel a fire building between us. When I kicked the door open, his lips twisted into a smirk.

Thor weaved his way through and crashed on the sofa.

Chance waved a finger at me and said, "You only want me for my tools, vixen."

I pulled him through the threshold. "That may be true, but not all your tools are tucked in your toolbox."

Chance scratched his head and stared at the demolition. "Care to explain?"

"I could…" I turned to stare at the pile of drywall and wood. I had tossed the nails earlier. "Or I could slip into something a lot less comfortable and explain it to you in Braille."

Chance kicked the door shut, hoisted me in his arms, and carried me to the bedroom.

Chapter 30

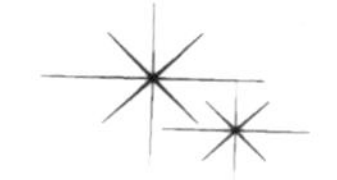

"Dogs feel very strongly that they should always go with you in the car, in case the need should arise for them to bark violently at nothing right in your ear."

—Dave Barry

I woke up before both Chance and Thor, anxious to find out what was written on those pages. I took a quick shower and climbed into a pair of running shorts, a T-shirt, and tennis shoes, foregoing the makeup. I twisted my hair into a clip and put on a pot of coffee. Then I took my findings and my own notebook out onto the front porch to read.

I first sifted through the folder. It didn't hold research or notes from my father's work as I had hoped. Instead, there were newspaper clippings about drug busts as far away as Kansas.

Teen arrested for intent to sell ecstasy in McHenry County
Student found beaten, unconscious at University of Missouri
Cocaine, $15,000 cash, seized at Pekin apartment
Counterfeit money circulating through Barrington

Grow house—discovered outside of Madison—torched
Kansas City state troopers pull over semi—find meth lab

I stopped and read that one.

Kansas City police officers say they have arrested a man after pursuing a suspected "rolling meth lab." Police say the suspects led them on a high-speed chase through the downtown area at ten o'clock Thursday evening. The alleged chase ceased when a second suspect jumped out of the moving vehicle and the truck came to a stop. Chemicals used to produce methamphetamine and several needles were found inside the vehicle. The name of the driver is expected to be released after charges are filed. The second suspect fled the scene. Police encourage anyone with information to call the tip line number at the bottom of the page.

The dates of the articles varied widely, but the last one was dated two years before my father's death. There were a couple of names listed in the cocaine bust, Timothy Steinhoffel and Gregory Davis. Neither rang a bell. The burning grow house was discovered in an abandoned warehouse with no arrests made. The name of the student who was attacked was Kyle Waubaowski, but the teen selling pills must have been underage.

So why was he clipping these? And was the man driving the semi in the meth arrest Cole Tripp?

I tapped my pen against the folder and thought about that. Were all of these articles related to Cole Tripp? Perhaps he was the one who fled the scene and he got good at slipping under the radar. Was he a relative of my dad's? A friend? My father didn't talk much about his past and I didn't ask. Being a happy kid with more than enough family, I never missed not having that second set of grand-parents. Although, I knew his parents had both died in a car crash when he was eighteen. He used the insurance money to put himself through school, where he met my mother and built the newspaper from the ground up.

What was this all about?

I sighed, put the file on the table next to me, and opened up the tiny pad of spiral-bound paper that had been neatly tucked inside.

A man came to me, claiming that I was in danger and I suspect RJ is behind it. The name changes throughout the years, but the crimes are always volatile. Drugs, thievery, forgery, violence. When we spoke two years ago, I vowed that it was the last penny I would ever give. And the last conversation I would ever agree to. I threatened exposure to the authorities, warned that I had the evidence, and I would use it. I would no longer protect a sociopath.

I have a family to protect. A loving wife and vibrant daughter who depend on me. They know nothing about RJ, and it's best that way. If they knew, it could only hurt them. So that is why I am burying all that I have—all that will protect my family from a maniac.

I have aided RJ as best I could, under the guise that it was my job to do so, although always the escape route is preplanned by my foster sibling. Those, I refuse to help execute.

But the crimes grow more sinister and the money is never enough. My conscience—once filled with guilt for being the blood child, the favorite child—can no longer justify my actions.

Oscar is the only one who knows about the wall. I requested to hide a "time capsule" here when we were renovating the cottage.

Lying, I told him it would be a gift for Stacy to unveil on her thirtieth birthday. I also plan to entrust him with a very valuable family heirloom, hidden inside a lockbox to be given to her on the same date.

One I hope her mother and I will give in person.

Inside that lockbox is—

"There you are."

I jumped halfway out of my skin as Chance came through the screen door.

"Hey, you all right?"

I shut the notebook and said, "Of course. Just going over some research."

He looked at me funny, kissed me, and said, "I'll call you later."

I watched as his truck kicked up dirt all over the driveway, wondering how many other secrets were waiting for me.

Thor came trotting through the door and immediately watered the lawn. I went inside to get some coffee and finish reading.

The rest of my father's notes indicated that the lockbox was to be put in my grandfather, Oscar's, private vault (which only he and his attorney, Stan Plough, have access to) and that it contained evidence to put RJ away. The combination was scribbled on the last page of the notebook.

This was his insurance policy. This was supposed to protect him from becoming RJ's next victim.

But it got him killed anyway.

I slammed my fist on the counter.

Who was this person? I didn't even know if RJ was male or female. How old? Had to be younger than my father. And who was the man who warned him?

Something snapped into place then.

Cole. Cole Tripp wanted me to know my father had been murdered. He must have been the one who visited him all those years ago. So he wasn't a friend of my dad's. He was a friend—or relative—of RJ.

After two more cups of coffee and a whole lot of brain racking it was time to take Keesha to the vet.

I shoved everything into my bag, checked to see if the Mace was there, tossed it in the car, and trekked over to the inn. I peeked through the back door first and saw Fiona at the stove.

The door was ajar. I slipped past the screen and quietly closed it. I said hello to Fiona and she greeted me with her usual singsong voice.

At least she wasn't angry.

"Is Keesha ready for her vet appointment?"

Fiona said, "She sure is. You better get a move-on before Birdie sees you. She's still a bit hot under the collar."

Of course. "Fiona, do you remember if my father ever had a relative named RJ?"

She was whisking eggs in a blue ceramic mixing bowl. "Doesn't ring a bell, dear."

"Thanks." I turned to the pretty collie curled up in the corner. "Come on, Keesha."

I was about to lead her out the back door when I heard the stairs creak, so I hightailed it through the hallway and into the parlor.

The whole band was there, sipping coffee. They looked more alert than they should have for working well into the night, except for the perpetually red-eyed Sebastian.

I greeted them cordially, careful not to touch them. I didn't need a migraine just then.

Becky let out a startled cry when she saw Keesha. Brian looked at her, concerned.

"Sorry," she said, hand on her chest. "She startled me. I'm afraid of dogs."

"I didn't know that," Rob said.

"There's a lot you don't know about me," Becky snapped.

"And more I wish I didn't," said Rob.

Rob. RJ? He looked harmless, like a manager for an Old Navy clothing store.

But so did Ted Bundy.

"I'm sorry, but can you take her out of the room? Please?" Becky asked.

"Oh, right, sure, sorry."

I led Keesha to the car and heard Thor crying from inside the house. There was enough room for both of them, and since Thor loved all the attention he got at the vet, I decided to bring him along. I was about to shut the hatchback when I noticed those goggles dangling from his mouth.

"Seriously?"

Thor shoved them into my hand.

"You know"—I strapped the goggles over is head and turned them on—"if you had thumbs you'd be the perfect animal."

Leo called on the way to the vet. "I just wanted you to know that the prints came back from the rig and there's a set on there that match Cole Tripp."

I almost dropped the phone. "No, that can't be."

"Prints don't lie."

"That makes no sense. Why would he tell me my father was murdered if he did it?"

"Guilty conscience. Guy serves time, finds Jesus, then confesses all his sins."

"But that would put him right back in the cage."

"Sometimes they have a hard time adjusting to life on the outside. Sometimes they want to go back."

I tapped the steering wheel. Was Cole RJ? Was he coming after me now? In the letter, Dad said there had been many aliases.

"Do you know if this guy ever used an alias?"

"Negative."

"Besides the explosion, was there any other history of violence on his record?"

Leo shuffled some papers around. "None."

"Look, I'm at the vet, can I call you later?"

"You know where to find me."

I disconnected and swung into the parking lot of the vet's office. It was located in the middle of a busy strip mall off the highway and there were a lot of cars pulling in and out of the slots. Morning commuters stopping for their coffee, people squeezing in eye doctor appointments before work, and fast-food junkies searching for a hot egg sandwich.

I leashed both dogs and let them out of the car. Keesha was still timid, but I managed to coax her inside with Thor's chivalrous aid.

Tracey, the thirtysomething assistant, gushed all over the big man the minute we entered, as Keesha stood politely by his side.

"Who wants a cookie?" Tracey sang. "Who wants a cookie?"

Thor barked and Tracey tossed him a peanut butter treat. He caught it in the air and happily chewed, spewing crumbs all over the carpet.

"And who is this?" Tracey asked, handing Keesha a cookie. Keesha shied away, but Thor, never one to turn down a meal, gobbled it up.

"This is the patient. Her name is Keesha and I'm afraid that's all I know. I found her in the park the other night."

"Aw, poor thing." Tracey scratched Keesha's ear, but the dog just gave her a forlorn look.

I was just happy she didn't ask how I knew the collie's name.

We discussed the checkup and my concerns and Tracey created a file. She carried the file down the brightly lit hallway where the examination rooms were situated.

Thor got to work picking up all the scents and smells from the carpet since his last checkup.

Tracey called us back and I told Thor to stay in the waiting room. He collapsed onto the carpet, all four legs taking up half the space.

Keesha kept pace alongside me as Tracey led us into the Rin Tin Tin room. There were pictures of the famous shepherd all over the walls and I read about his history as a war hero while I waited for Dr. Zimmerman.

A few minutes later, Dr. Zimmerman entered the room.

"Hi, Stacy."

"Hey, Doc."

He glanced over his assistant's brief notes, then washed his meaty hands. He was a burly man who looked more like a professional wrestler than a veterinarian, which was the main reason I chose him to be Thor's doctor. He had the muscle to lift my two-hundred-pound dog, should the occasion arise.

"How's Thor?"

"Great."

"Laying off the cheeseburgers?"

"He prefers hot dogs now."

The good doctor shook his head, scolding me with his eyes.

"Sparingly."

He nodded like I was full of it. Which I was.

He weighed Keesha, checked her ears, eyes, and temperature, dictating notes to Tracey. I explained that she was lost from her family, but also seemed lethargic.

"It could be dietary, but we can do a quick radiograph to make sure nothing's broken or fractured. If it looks like there's a problem, a closer x-ray would be the next step." He looked at her gums and said, "We should scan her for a microchip."

Tracey rushed out to grab whatever they used for that. She was back in a flash, carrying what looked like a garage door opener with a screen on it. She held it up near Keesha's neck and read the results.

Tracey raised her eyebrows. "Well, this is a new one."

"Who does she belong to?" I asked.

"Joliet Correctional Facility."

Chapter 31

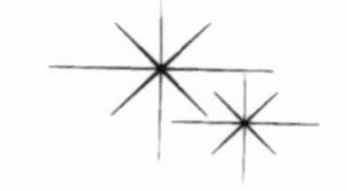

"Dogs are not our whole life,
but they make our lives whole."
—Roger Caras

Well, my day just got more complicated.

Tracey explained that a lot of prisons have implemented dog training programs. Sister Pauline Quinn began the program back in 1981 at the Washington State Correctional Center for Women. The organization rescues pets from kill shelters and, with the help of qualified trainers, teaches inmates how to properly care for and prepare an animal for service with the disabled or just to be a well-adjusted family pet.

"It's a win-win, because often the prisoners are transformed by the experience of being unconditionally loved and respected, not to mention the joy of doing something that's important and the feeling of hope that comes with it," Tracey had said.

I dialed the number to the facility while Keesha was being radiographed.

I spoke with a nice woman who said that indeed, Keesha was one of their dogs, and that she had been adopted by the recently freed Cole Tripp.

"They live with these dogs twenty-four seven, you see." She had a bold voice like a basketball coach. "The crates are kept right inside the cell with the inmates and their sole responsibility is to train these animals for six weeks. Cole had been a part of our program since its inception five years ago. We don't usually allow violent offenders into the program, but since his crimes were mostly drug related, despite the accident that killed the woman, he was permitted in on a trial basis."

"Wow, so he was doing this for five years. That's a long time."

"He was very good at it. There's something magical about watching a hardened, tattooed man rolling around on the floor baby-talking to a dog."

"I can imagine."

"Keesha was his last trainee, and since he did such good for the program, we permitted him to take her home. So do you know Cole? Is Keesha lost?"

I hesitated for a moment. The woman was doing the work of angels. She deserved the truth and I told her. "But don't worry, Keesha is safe and she's in a good home right now," I said.

She choked back a tear, paused, and said, "Well, I'm glad to hear that." She excused herself and hung up.

I didn't know how to feel at that moment. Sorry for Keesha, sorry for Cole, but mostly angry at whoever would hurt him for trying to straighten out his life and do the right thing.

I was also pretty damn certain he didn't run down my father.

The doctor came into the lobby then, Keesha trailing behind. "She certainly ate something she shouldn't have, but it's small. It should pass in her stool. She'll feel better when that's over."

I thanked him, paid the bill, and left.

I loaded Thor into the backseat first and ran back inside to fetch Keesha. We were striding toward my car when my bag slipped off my shoulder, spilling my keys onto the pavement. I loosened the leash for a moment and bent to get the keys as they slid near the sewer drain.

"No, not now!"

They didn't tumble over the edge, thankfully.

That was when I noticed I had dropped the leash. And out of nowhere an older model red sedan came barreling through the parking lot right at Keesha.

"Keesha!"

She stood there, frightened out of her mind and shaking as I dove to push her out of the careening car's path.

The car screeched off and Thor bolted through the open window, giving chase.

"THOR! NO! COME, BOY!"

Tracey came rushing through the door and said, "Are you all right? My goodness, people should be more careful."

"Take her!" I threw Keesha's lead at her and sprinted in the direction Thor had gone—around the building and down a back alley.

My adrenaline was pumping and my heart was in my throat. The fear and panic of knowing that I might turn the corner to find my dog bloody—or worse—sent me flying around the corner.

He was sitting near a bicycle rack, panting like crazy, but unharmed.

"That was bad! Bad dog, Thor!"

I rushed over to him and squeezed him tight, his goggles pressing into the side of my cheek.

I pulled back. Looked at his spy wear.

If I had known, before he entered my life, how much smarter this dog was than me, I would have been completely intimidated.

Instead, I was just glad he was on my side.

I made a quick stop at home, stocked up on water and dog food, then slipped into a pair of flair jeans, strapped Cinnamon's gun around my ankle, and left.

Mace was no match for four thousand pounds of steel bearing down on you.

And I'll be a witch in hell before I let someone hurt my dogs.

Next, I went to the newspaper office to figure out how the hell to work these goggles.

"Well, nice of you to join us," Parker said.

I held up my hand. "Not now."

Parker didn't say anything more as I marched past him.

Derek was on the phone when I walked in with Thor and Keesha, but he quickly cut the call. Must have been the look on my face. I unfastened the spy wear around

Thor's head, handed it to him, and said, "How do I retrieve the data?"

"Good morning to you too, sunshine."

I glared at him.

"I hate that look."

"Then don't make me toss it at you."

"Did you get another dog?"

"She's a guest."

Derek shrugged his shoulders, reached over and grabbed the goggles, flipped open a latch, and inserted a USB cable. Next, he inserted the other end into his computer and downloaded the video onto his laptop.

We watched several minutes of scenery, sniffing of crotches, poop, melted ice cream on the sidewalk, and the sashay of an Afghan's ass.

Finally I said, "Derek, fast forward. If there's a time stamp, it would be around the 9:15 mark that I'm looking for."

Derek moved the video forward several hours until I said, "Freeze!"

He paused the frame. "Hey, that reminds me, we're all going to Tastee Freez for lunch. You in?"

"Nope."

"Why not?"

"Things to do." People to kill.

"Man, why can't you be a team player?"

I ignored that and asked, "Can you zoom the screen?"

Derek made the screen bigger and I thanked him. I wrote down the license plate of the maniac who tried to mow down Keesha.

I thanked Derek and he said, "Hey, Sydney called. That file is ready. Pick it up anytime. His fee might be a bit pricey since it was no easy task creating an .mp3 file from that older model equipment. Did you want the watch back?"

"Yes, will you tell him I'll be there this afternoon?"

Derek said he would do that, and he put the video from the doggie cam on an external disk and handed it to me.

I told Parker I was following a lead and that I'd be back right after I talked to Leo. He waved from his open office door and I drove to the police station with the disk in my pocket.

I realize it may not have been the smartest move—walking into a cop shop with a weapon that didn't belong to me clinging to my ankle—but right now, I was desperate.

Leo was talking to Amy when I entered the building. He looked at Thor, then at Keesha and said, "I see you are traveling with an entourage these days."

"I'm keeping up my end of the deal. I want you to keep up yours."

He opened his arms and stepped aside, allowing the three of us to pass. "Come on in."

I handed him the drive as he settled into his chair. "What's this?"

"This is video of someone trying to kill Keesha." I pointed to the fluffy collie and she rested her head against Thor.

"Why would someone want to kill a dog?" Leo asked. He flipped on his monitor and plugged the external disk into the USB port.

"That's your job, Chief."

Leo smirked and said, "You're right. Okay, let's check it out."

He frowned after a few minutes and I said, "Oh yeah. You have to fast forward. Thor got the goggles yesterday and I didn't know how to unload the data."

"Thor?"

I swung around and leaned over his shoulder. "Wait, stop! There." I pointed to the image of the car driving away.

"This looks a lot like Thor chasing cars."

I sighed. "Leo, just run the plates, please. I swear to you, this car tried to plow Keesha down and I want to know why."

I explained to him the connection between Keesha and Cole. I didn't tell him about my father's time capsule because, really, what would I say? *Yes, we're looking for a person named RJ.* Might not go over well.

He seemed intrigued then. He plugged in some numbers into his computer and said, after a minute or so, "It's a rental car." He picked up the phone, chatted with someone on the other end, thanked her, and hung up. He stared at the phone for several seconds.

"Well? Who rented it?"

Leo looked me straight in the eye and said, "Cole Tripp."

Chapter 32

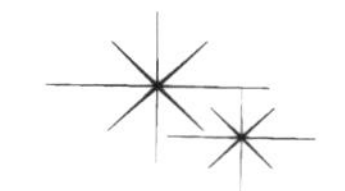

Leo called out a search on the car and I left the police station to head to the spy store, really hoping Cole Tripp was not a zombie.

Sydney was behind the counter when I pushed through the door.

"Hi, Sydney, Derek said you had something for me?"

He grinned. "This was a doozy, I tell you, had to do a lot of data configuring to update the technology, but I think you're all set."

"You think?"

Sydney said, "Of course, I don't actually listen to the contents. That would be a violation of the confidentiality agreement I provide to all my customers."

"Of course," I said.

"What kind of phone do you have?"

I showed it to him.

"Would you like me to upload it here?"

"That would be great."

I handed Sydney my phone and browsed the store for a little bit, choosing a few items for myself I thought would come in handy.

After a few minutes, Sydney rang me up and I was out the door, with my purchases stuffed in my bag. It was a twenty-minute drive back, so I let both dogs out and walked them up the block to a grassy patch where they could do their business. Then I purchased two waters from a vending machine, grabbed the water dish from the car, and filled it.

They each took turns lapping up the water, Thor dripping half of his all over poor Keesha's head. I grabbed a towel from the backseat and wiped her down.

Her eyes were so soulful, she seemed half-human. I wanted to put her in my pocket and keep her safe.

Then the most amazing thing happened. She licked my hand.

My heart melted and we looked at each other for a few minutes longer. She cocked her head as if trying to read my thoughts and I did the same.

Except I was not Fiona.

But I did have something that might help figure this all out.

My notebook was buried beneath the pregnancy test packages, the purchases from the spy store, and my audio recorder. I dug it out, tossed the test packages in a nearby garbage can, and flipped to the page where I had recorded Fiona's reading notes from her session with the petite, furry girl.

Keesha
Pretty
Girl

Smart
Help
Teach
Show
Fun
Car
Lady
Bad
Man
Sad

Nope. All it revealed was her experience as a prison dog. The last three words I assumed meant it was bad what happened to Cole and she was sad about it.

I have learned over the years that sometimes, in order to figure out how the story ends, you must go back to the beginning.

So that's what we did.

I played the recording in the car on the drive back. It was fuzzy, but I could make out most of what was said.

I can't just kill a man in cold blood. You have to get that out of your head. Besides, you always said everything he touched turned to gold. Why don't you just hit him up for another payoff?

The voice from the phone call. Cole's voice.

Then, another.

He won't do it. I tried. That bastard owes me. Besides, we need the money if we're going to build another lab.

No way. I'm done with that. Let's just stick with the plan, RJ. This gig I got going now with stealing the trailers is going to be good money. The VINs are legit and the buyer in Chicago is a sure thing. We'll be fine. Remember what Dad always said, stick with the sure thing and don't get caught.

Dad got caught, Cole. That's why we ended up in the system in the first place.

Look, I've been on probation for two years. If I get busted again, I'm looking at hard time. Only thing that saved me was they couldn't prove we had distributed.

The money is all gone. We need this. We hit him and I know I can use that as leverage.

With who? Look, you said he knows too much. He may have told someone what he's got on you.

Not a chance. He's afraid of me.

Well, what if he changes his mind?

A pause.

What? What are you looking at?

Dead men tell no tales.

What are you doing? Stop it! Get your hands off the wh—

A crash, the sickening sound of metal crunching against metal.

And that was all.

I was shaking with fury as we made our way down to the lake, my resolve stronger than ever.

Thor took off after an unsuspecting rabbit and Keesha and I wandered around the embankment. It was cloudy today, cooler than yesterday, but my blood was boiling hot.

There had to be something here. Something I missed.

I followed Keesha as she sniffed around the trees and pranced through the sand, my focus on the dog's actions and energy.

She inspected a dead fish, pawed at it a bit. We moved on to some wildflowers, a willow tree, and a fallen log.

I closed my eyes for a moment, sending a message to Cole to present himself.

I waited.

He didn't show.

I walked closer to the water and tried to call him again.

That was when the white tiger appeared.

And behind me, a branch cracked.

I turned, expecting to see Thor.

Instead, I was staring at a crossbow.

Chapter 33

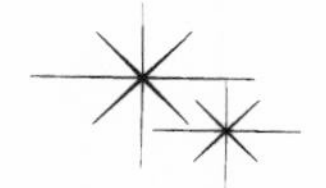

"The poor dog, in life the firmest friend, The first to welcome, foremost to defend."

—Lord Byron

I dove behind a tree and an arrow pierced the bark. Another whooshed toward me and I scrambled back around, but I wasn't fast enough. It sliced across my hip, and the ripping pain doubled me over. The gun was in a holster strapped to my ankle, but I was afraid by the time I retrieved it I would have an arrow in my back. I stood there, perfectly still, wondering what my next move should be.

Then, it was made for me.

"Come out of there or I'll kill the dog."

Keesha? Where was she? Or was it Thor?

I took a long, deep breath and limped around to face Becky.

"I take it you're a fan of the *Hunger Games* too, huh, RJ?"

"You're pretty observant. And smart. Do yourself a favor and be smart now. I'm taking the dog. Make a move and I'll kill you."

She trained the bow on me with one hand and walked toward Keesha.

I scanned the woods, the lake. No sign of anyone near. Nowhere to run.

"You killed your blood brother. How could you do that?"

"Because he was going to rat me out. Rats deserve to die."

I heard a rustling above me as a squirrel scurried down the tree. "My father didn't deserve to die. He told no one about you. I guess you're less significant than you think."

She snorted. "Psychobabble doesn't work on me."

"Right, I forgot you're a sociopath."

She snorted again and said, "Sticks and stones. He thought he was so much better than me. Thought he could say *no* to me. I deserved that inheritance from Mr. and Mrs. Perfect and they didn't leave me a goddamn dime! I earned that money!"

What was that supposed to mean? She earned it?

A trace of something crossed her brow. A flicker of movement from the corner of her eye.

Her own face betraying her because she had said too much.

"You killed them, didn't you?" I said.

She stared me down, deadpanned. Didn't say a word.

"You're a monster."

Her grip tightened on the bow. This wasn't just anyone in a desperate situation. She truly was out of her mind.

"Sticks and stones."

Stones. There was a giant rock nearby. If I was fast enough…

In front of me, Keesha crouched to release her bowels.

RJ stared at the dog, eyes wide. She had two arrows left.

She flung the bow over her shoulder and lunged for Keesha.

"Leave her alone, you crazy bitch!"

I dove after RJ, but the collie charged away.

Except it wasn't the dog the woman was aiming for, it was what Keesha had deposited in the sand. That's when I knew and I scrambled for it too.

The radiograph, the broken letters on her custom-made tambourine—was that the weapon used to hit Cole on the head? Keesha must have eaten one of the letters that spelled out *Nevermore.*

Which would place them both at the scene of the crime.

We fought over the feces and RJ got in a good closed-fist crack to my jaw. I grabbed the back of her head and shoved her face in the sand and Keesha's contribution to it, but she wrestled away and elbowed me between the shoulder blades.

I saw something shiny then and I grabbed for it.

That's when RJ shoved me hard and flipped to reach for her bow. I shuffled for the gun on my ankle, but the maniac stomped on my wrist and I screamed in agony.

She sprung to her feet and I delivered a roundhouse kick that took her down again.

I flipped my pant leg up and unsnapped the holster on the gun.

But I was too late.

The bow was aimed directly at my heart.

Then, from the rocks above, I heard the low, deadly growl of an animal about to attack.

We both turned to see Thor perched on a boulder, two-inch canines dripping saliva.

He lunged before RJ had time to redirect her aim. The dog came down on top of her, hard. The arrow misfired and stuck in the damp earth below the boulder.

The impact sent Thor and my attacker tumbling through the sand.

I shuffled to my feet, turned, and told Keesha, "Go!" And grabbed the letter. Shoved it in my pocket.

The collie darted off into the forest and I spun back around.

What happened next took place in slow motion

RJ aimed the bow at my Great Dane.

I screamed in terror, reached for my gun.

But I was too late.

My familiar—my pet, my friend—crashed into the water.

Lifeless.

The sound of a demon escaped my throat and I tackled RJ, beating her face raw with my bare hands.

Tears streamed down my checks, mixed with feces, blood, and sand as I delivered blow after merciless blow to a woman I had just met.

The rage, hurt, and scars of fourteen years of loss and agony I unleashed on this one individual.

I couldn't stop myself.

Then, in the distance, a tiger roared.

Closer, a horse whinnied.

A shy dog barked in protest.

It was the animals who brought me back to reality.

I jumped up and sprinted to Thor.

There are stories where, under duress, people find the strength of ten men. Mothers lifting cars off children. Men hauling cranes off coworkers.

That was the only explanation for what happened on the beach that day, although I don't remember it.

I was told they found me trying to carry Thor into the vet's office, the arrow still sticking out of his ribs. Tracey helped me lay him on the floor before she sprinted for the vet.

Doc Zimmerman came rushing out of an exam room. He took one look at me and said, "We'll fix him." He called someone to help and they carried Thor into the back area of the clinic.

He wouldn't allow me to stay in the room through the surgery, so I washed up in the bathroom, feeling numb. That part, I remember.

I found some bandages for my hip in the medicine cabinet. Dressed the wound.

The waiting room of any doctor's office or hospital is purgatory on earth. Waiting to hear if your loved ones will live or die. Waiting to hear if your life is about to change. If there will be a void when you leave there.

Waiting for answers.

I sat there, feeling helpless, while a thousand voices rambled through my head. Voices I tried to turn off, but who wouldn't be ignored.

Because there was a piece of the puzzle still missing.

"You always said everything he touched turned to gold."

"Dead men tell no tales."

Grow house—discovered outside of Madison—torched

"Your father was murdered."

Kansas City state troopers pull over semi-truck—find meth lab

"Look, I've been on probation for two years."

Two years. Something was niggling my mind about that number. Two years.

And then it hit me.

Tracey interrupted my thoughts. "He's going to be fine. The arrow went about an inch deep. It sliced a muscle, so he'll have internal and external stitches, but after he's patched up, he'll make a full recovery."

I thanked Tracey, asked her to kennel Keesha, and told her to call me the minute Thor woke up.

I dialed Leo's private number from the car.

"There's a woman who was beaten up at Eagle Lake. You might want to get over there."

"Where are you?"

"On my way to kill my boss."

Chapter 34

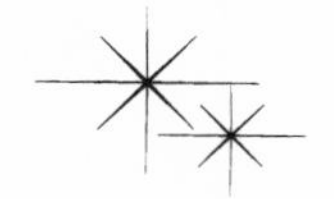

"It's not the size of the dog in the fight,
it's the size of the fight in the dog."
—Mark Twain

I marched into Parker's office and shut the door. Closed all the blinds.

He looked up from the computer and frowned at me. "You smell like shit. Literally."

"Why did you move here from Madison?"

Parker shrugged. "A fresh start."

"Because someone torched your grow house?"

"What?"

The raw look on his face told me everything I needed to know and I trained my gun on him.

"Hey, Stacy, take it easy. Put that thing away before someone gets hurt."

"See, that's the thing, Parker. Someone already got hurt."

"What are you talking about?"

"You know what I'm talking about!" I yelled. "Everything he touched turned to gold. Isn't that what you said? Where did you hear that, Shea? Where?"

He stood, moved around to the side of his desk, and I followed.

"RJ, perhaps?" I said.

My soon-to-be-dead boss swallowed hard. "Stacy, you have to understand, she's crazy. For Christ's sake, she tried to set me on fire."

"He trusted you and you betrayed him!" I didn't think it was possible to get any angrier, but I did. It was like a snake pit festering in my belly. The gun shook in my hand.

Shea wagged his head. "No. I tried to warn him."

"LIAR!" I shoved his monitor off the desk and it crashed onto the carpet.

He stared at the broken glass and his shoulders heaved. "Okay, at first, I admit, I was a plant. She sent me here to stake out your father, find out what his next business venture would be, but"—he looked at me, his eyes pleading—"then I got to know him. And your mother. And you."

I held the gun steady, the grip engulfed in my hand, and pointed it at his head. Parker took a step back and I moved forward. We circled the desk.

"She thought the newspaper would be a moneymaker." His words came out like rapid fire then. "I showed her the books, explained that it wasn't the gold mine she thought. Then I didn't hear from her for two years. She found some other guy or something and set her sights elsewhere."

"So you were lovers?"

He nodded.

"Then why did you stay?"

"I liked it here. I liked your dad, the town. It felt good to be legitimate. My old life seemed like a distant nightmare. Plus"—he looked at me—"I thought if she ever returned we could face her together. It seemed like there was nothing your father and I couldn't accomplish."

The white tiger flashed in the photo on the wall, a warning, a reminder. *Don't go too far.*

I yanked the frame from the nail and smashed it on the floor.

I wrapped both hands around the grip of the gun. "Get on your knees."

He shook his head, but he did it.

I stepped closer. "Give me one good reason I shouldn't kill you."

The door flew open at that moment. "Stacy! Drop the gun."

The voice was Leo's.

I ignored him. Didn't even look at him, my mind was only focused on the truth.

Parker looked toward the door, hope in his eyes. Then he saw my face and the hope drained.

Good. Now he knew how I felt.

"Don't do this," Leo said.

"I didn't know she came back, I swear," said Parker, hands in the air.

"LIAR!" Both my hands hugged the gun, my finger perched on the trigger.

"It's true! I swear. He told me he had something important to do when he left that night. Gave me a lockbox and said to hang onto it until the morning. But he never made it in that next day."

Parker was quivering and I was enjoying it.

"So I hid the box in the floorboard of his car after the crash. I didn't know what else to do with it. If it had something to do with RJ, I wanted to bury it with your father. Certainly, it wouldn't do any good if your mother or you got a hold of it."

"Why? Why did RJ do it?"

"Do what?"

"I have a tape, Parker. I know who crashed the truck into my father's car."

He paused too long for my taste. "WHY?"

Parker licked his lips and his eyes scanned in the direction of Leo. "There was one thing. One way she could cash in on one last scam. But I didn't know what she had in mind before the crash, I swear. And I'm so ashamed." He sobbed.

Shea looked at the broken picture of him and my dad holding the award. Together.

Partners.

And the last piece clicked into place.

We hit him and I know I can use that as leverage.

With who?

"Insurance money," I said, venom on my tongue. "You inherited Dad's half of the paper. There must have been a payout when he died."

"It wasn't much. But she promised never to come back if I gave it to her. She left me a PO box number. When I got the check, I cashed it and sent every cent to her. I wanted her to stay out of my life, out of yours."

"Stacy, put the goddamn gun down. Don't do something you'll regret," Leo said. "We'll sort it all out."

I almost did.

Almost.

But another thought occurred to me.

"You shot at me," I said slowly. "You didn't go fishing that day."

Parker started sweating profusely. "Just to scare you. It wasn't a real gun."

"You were the guy with the BB gun?" Leo asked.

Parker kept his gaze on me. "I did it to protect you. When Leo asked me about the phone call to the office from the dead man's phone, I knew it had something to do with RJ. If she thought you had any dirt on her, dirt I know your dad warned her about, she would have killed you."

"You could have hurt me or Derek. You could have blinded either of us, maybe even killed us!"

Parker shook his head. "I missed on purpose, but that bird flew at me and the last few shots misfired. I didn't want to hurt anyone." He shook his head and tears fell.

"And Scoog?"

Leo said, "He had a heart attack, Stacy."

"But you were there, weren't you, Parker?"

"I didn't mean to scare him," he said quietly. "He had the record of me looking for the car after Stacy Senior died. I didn't want anyone to find it. His arm just came off in my hand."

"And then you set it up to look like he was berry picking."

Parker looked down. Another sob escaped his throat and my heart hardened further.

He had no right to cry.

"Come on, Stacy," Leo said. "Please, let's just go."

I looked at Leo. Looked at Parker. Studied the shattered glass of the picture frame.

I sighed and shook my head. To Shea I said, "You're not worth it."

Slowly I lowered the gun.

Leo and Parker each blew out a breath.

I watched as my boss rose from his knees.

But I thought better of it and fired at him anyway.

Chapter 35

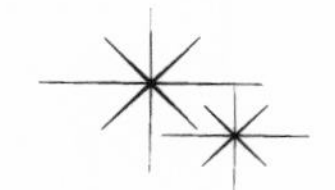

The electricity from the taser lit up Parker like a Christmas tree. I watched him convulse for a moment, flopping around like a fish on land.

Leo looked at me, incredulous. "A taser gun?"

I shrugged. "Gotta love that spy store."

"I could have killed you."

I said, "No, you couldn't."

Then I left.

Chapter 36

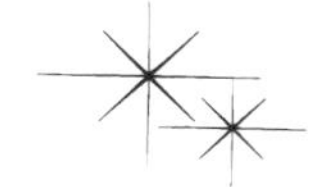

On the morning of the summer solstice, with the sun shining and the cardinals singing, I found myself back in the cemetery speaking to my father.

"You can rest easy, Dad. RJ can't hurt anyone anymore. And Parker, well, he'll likely face charges too. Leo is sorting the whole mess now. He's been questioning your old partner for a few days, not to mention a couple of the band members. The chief is convinced that Rebecca Jean couldn't have rowed Cole out to the lake to dump him by herself. Knowing what she's capable of, though, I have no doubts she acted alone."

Leo had the "e" that Keesha had swallowed and then eliminated, proving that RJ, at the very least, made contact with her blood brother. I suspected the raven medallion would match that "unique" impression on the back of the man's head too, though it was doubtful it had the power to knock him unconscious. She must have hit him with something else after she stunned him. That, coupled with the evidence inside the lockbox, and her attack on me, should be enough to put her away for a long time.

He also said that Gramps was aware of the false wall I had knocked down (I turned the article clippings over to Leo), but that he never knew of any lockbox.

"There was something in there for you," he told me. "It's gift wrapped with instructions for you to open on your thirtieth birthday."

The family heirloom, I presumed. I told him to give it to Gramps for safekeeping as my father had intended.

I didn't need any more surprises for a while.

I said to my father's headstone now, "I need one last favor, Dad." I pulled out the penny from the year Lolly was to be wed. Fiona had any number of pennies stashed away for emergencies such as this. They are a great conductor to contact the spirits.

I put the coin to my third eye and imagined Lolly in her wedding dress, a faceless groom standing by her side.

I didn't dare do any further magic in this place.

I set the coin on my father's headstone and said, "I made a promise to Aunt Lolly to find out what happened to her beloved Jack. Think you could help out with that?"

A long while passed.

Then, behind me, I heard a familiar voice. Then another and another.

Mr. Scoog spoke first. "Take it easy on the girl, folks, she had quite an ordeal last time. We don't want to break her." He looked at me and said, "You're a legend around here, you know. Did a lot of good for the dead."

I nodded.

"So now we'll do something for you."

The crowd parted slowly and there, holding a beer bottle that read *Lolly's Lager,* was a young, handsome ghost.

The remaining spirits misted away and I approached Jack.

He had sparkling eyes and quite the physique. I could see why my aunt was drawn to him. He fumbled with the label on the beer, peeling it back and forth.

Finally he spoke. "How is she?"

"She's fine. She misses you."

"I miss her too." A cloud swooped across his face. "Tell her I'm sorry."

"I think she knows."

He stared at the statue of the Virgin Mary for a long time. Sat on a cement bench.

"What happened to you?" I asked.

He shook his head. "It was foolish. I wasn't careful."

"Go on," I urged.

"I was preparing a special lager just for her." He held up his beer to show me the label. There was a silhouette of a woman beneath the scrolling font. "She could hold her liquor like no other."

That did not surprise me.

"Anyway, I was mixing it in an old corner of the brewery that had been walled off from the inside. It was a circular stone structure like a silo. I had to lower the supplies down pretty carefully, but it was going to be worth it just to see the surprise on her face when I unveiled it for the wedding. I didn't tell anyone, you see. Wanted it to be a secret."

He took a swig of the potion. "I worked on it for months. Up and down that ladder every day." He stopped to watch a pair of doves flutter through the trees. "On the morning of the wedding, I was hauling up the first case when I slipped and broke my neck."

"And no one knew to look for you there."

Jack nodded.

"Where was the brewery?"

"It was on my grandfather's land. Off Blue Diamond Road."

"Your cousin lives there now. He's a metal sculptor."

Jack nodded. "It's good that it's still in the family." He took another swig of beer. "So you'll tell her?"

"I will. And we'll find you a proper resting spot."

With that, he smiled and faded into a whisper on the wind, but the beer bottle remained, clanking in the absence of a hand. It up-righted itself when a breeze blew by. A flash of crimson flew in front of me, circled over my head then, and landed on top of the bottle.

A cardinal.

I made a quick stop to the vet's office to see how Keesha was doing. Tracey decided to adopt her and she was presently the office mascot.

She wiggled over to me, happily shaking her tail, and I gave her a big smooch on her heart-shaped head. I promised a playdate with Thor as soon as he was all better. She yipped in agreement and scampered off.

Thor was recovering quietly at home, with as many cheeseburgers and hot dogs as he wanted. The wound was healing nicely, thanks to Doc Zimmerman and the magical touch of Fiona.

When I got to the cottage, he was sprawled across the couch, upside down, watching *America's Funniest Videos.*

The holiday ceremonies were to begin in an hour, so I was applying eyeliner when Chance arrived.

"Hey, it's me," he called. "Don't come out guns ablazing." He walked into the bathroom and whistled at me. "You look gorgeous."

"Thank you."

There was a bouquet of thyme, lavender, rosemary, and sage in his hand tied up in a pretty ribbon.

"For you, m'lady." He bowed.

"Thank you, how sweet. I'll put them in water."

I walked into the kitchen, chatting about how I thought it might be time to plant my own garden in the back so I wouldn't have to swipe herbs from Birdie.

When I turned around, he was on one knee.

"What are you doing?" I shook my head. "Chance, get up."

He grabbed my hand. "I was going to do this later, but I decided it should be private."

"No, later is good," I stammered. Much later. Much, much later.

"Stacy, I love you. I love everything about you. I love your wit, your smile, your loyalty, your determination."

Oh God.

"I think you're the most exciting, compassionate woman I've ever met."

No, no, no.

"And I want to spend the rest of my life making you happy."

He pulled out a ring. A modest cut emerald.

It was exactly what I would have chosen.

"Chance, I—"

"Will you marry me?"

I swallowed hard. "We haven't even been together that long."

"We've known each other most of our lives."

His face was sincere, so very sweet.

"I just think it's too soon."

He shrugged, still on his knee. "Maybe, but things are different now."

"What things?"

"You know." He put his hand on my belly. "The baby," he said softly.

"What? I'm not pregnant!"

"You're not?"

"No."

"Oh." He looked confused. "I saw you buy two pregnancy tests. I was on my way home from a job, stopped to get a soda at a convenience store." He gave me a sheepish look. "I didn't say anything because I thought maybe you wanted to keep it a secret for the time being. Superstitions do run strong with the Geraghty women, after all."

I grabbed his cheeks and kissed him. I did not deserve this man. "Oh, Chance"—I shook my head—"that was for Cinnamon."

He looked surprised for a moment. Then he said, "So what? Marry me anyway."

I turned down the proposal, gave back the ring. I couldn't agree to marry him. Not now. Not when there was one more very important thing to do.

That evening, after the wine was poured and the fire started, my grandmother approached me. We stood there in silence for a moment.

"You know why I did it, don't you?"

"Yes."

"Tell me."

"You wanted me to stand on my own this time. Because if I didn't learn now, I wouldn't be prepared for my mother's retrieval."

"Very good. How did you figure it out?"

"Your son was a cop. I don't expect you're all that gun shy."

She smiled, wistfully. "Are you prepared to begin your training? To learn more about your ancestors?"

"You mean the red-haired, fair-skinned magical people called the Tuatha Dé Danann?" I sipped my wine. "Ready as I'll ever be."

Birdie nodded, her red cape slipping just over her forehead.

I glanced at Lolly, clutching her lost groom's gift. And Fiona, gently stroking Thor. Then I looked down at my own glittering blue cape, wondering if any of the Danann's gifts belonged to our tribe.

Wondering if the months of training that lay ahead would prepare me for the next journey.

"They better," Birdie said. "Because it's the most important mission of your life."

I hated it when she did that. "And if I fail?"

"Neither you nor your mother will return home."

"Well, at least there's no pressure."

THE END

Author's Note

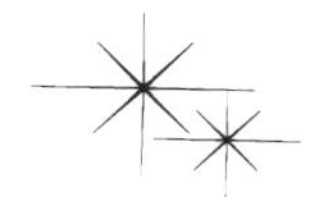

While writers often take great liberties in fiction, we also strive to make the reading experience as authentic as possible. Much of what you've read here came from hours of research. In case you're interested in further information, I've included links below to some of the highlights of the story you just read.

The Hill of Tara is located in County Meath, Ireland, and was the ceremonial epicenter for the seat of high kings. This is just one of many impressive ancient sites and has been the focus of many archeological digs over the years. Myths and rumors surround this sacred site, which is older than the pyramids of Egypt.

You will learn more about it—and other spiritual enclaves—in *Emerald Isle,* Stacy's next adventure.

The godlike people known as the Tuatha Dé Danann are to Ireland what King Arthur's legend is to England. Their gifts to the land and her people were many, with the four treasures being the most sacred. The ancient text *The Book of Invasions* highlights their journey in detail. It was compiled in the twelfth century by Irish monks.

Finally, the prison dog program has been adopted by many correctional facilities across the globe. It's been an invaluable tool to not only save the lives of dogs who otherwise would have been euthanized, but also the spirits of men and women who have lost their way. You can do a Google search to find out if there is a program in your area and how you can support it. The blog below has some great information and videos so you can see for yourself what a profound impact this program has on the lives of both four-legged and two-legged souls.

http://prisondogs.blogspot.com/

LITHA

This book takes place before the summer solstice, or Litha, when the sun is at the zenith of its power. It's the longest day of the year and is celebrated by pagans with a large bonfire to ward off evil spirits. This practice is called "setting the watch." Revelers jump through the fire for purification and good luck and often toss in herbs sacred to the day, such as rue, roses, and St. John's wort.

The word "solstice" is Latin for "sun stand still," which is precisely what appears to happen every year on the summer solstice. Usually the date is June 21, the first day of summer, according to our calendars. However, the longest day of the year technically falls when the sun has entered the Tropic of Cancer. Past cultures have viewed this time as Midsummer, or the middle of the growing season. After this date, the sun moves through the waning stage, days shorten, and winter approaches.

Midsummer's Eve is also charged with magic and prime time for casting spells. Pagans feel that this night is ripe for love charms, so couples jump over the flames of the bonfires to strengthen their bond and maidens tuck sprigs of yarrow under their pillows, hoping to lure suitors. Herbs plucked on Midsummer's Eve are thought to be at their peak for mystical purposes and ready for enchantment. As the veil thins between this and the Otherworld, it is also thought that one can see fairies dancing by rubbing a sprig of thyme on the eyelids. Often, folks linger all through the night drinking mead and ale, hoping to spot a fairy.

Midsummer marks the beginning of the waning sun, perfect to rid yourself of bad habits or negative traits—in other words, banishment rituals. Try this: while the fire is still hot, take a dark-colored piece of paper and write down the habit you wish to dispense. Fold the paper three times and toss it onto the coals, envisioning the heat burning away the negativity.

THE STORY OF DEMETER AND HELIOS

Demeter was the Greek goddess of Mother Earth. When her daughter, Persephone, was kidnapped, she turned to Helios, the all-seeing sun god, for answers. He informed her that it was Hades, god of the Underworld, who had taken Persephone. In anger, Demeter withdrew her services as an Earth mother and the plants began to wither and die while Demeter searched for Persephone, who emerged months later. When Persephone returned, Demeter tended to the

Earth once again. This was the Greeks' explanation for the harshness of winter and the spring thaw.

RECIPES FOR THE SUMMER SOLSTICE

Tomato-Cucumber Salad

Vine-ripened tomatoes and fleshy cucumbers are staples of the summer harvest. Pluck these veggies at their peak and before the critters steal them. If you don't have a garden patch, venture out to the nearest farmer's market. It's a world of difference from store-bought varieties.

2 medium cucumbers, sliced thick and halved
2 large tomatoes, quartered
½ medium red onion, chopped
8 ounces plain yogurt
1 tablespoon lemon juice
½ teaspoon sugar
1 tablespoon chopped fresh mint

In a medium bowl, toss together first three ingredients. Set aside. Mix thoroughly yogurt, lemon juice, sugar, and mint. Fold into cucumber mixture and chill for 30 minutes.

Grilled Sweet Potatoes

The vibrant orange of sweet potatoes reflect the hue of a late-summer sun, making them a perfect addition to a summer solstice celebration.

2 large sweet potatoes, peeled and sliced
1 teaspoon cumin
2 tablespoons brown sugar
¼ cup butter

Fire up the grill. Tear off two sheets of heavy-duty foil. Divide potatoes in half, placing each batch on top of a piece of foil. Sprinkle ½ teaspoon of cumin and 1 tablespoon of brown sugar over potatoes on each foil sheet. Divide butter. Dot each potato mixture with butter. Seal tightly. Double wrap, if needed. Place potato packets on grill and cook over medium heat for 40 minutes, turning occasionally.

Pomegranate-Chili Chicken

Ancient Greeks believed that the love goddess, Aphrodite, planted the first pomegranate seed on the island of Cyprus. The Chinese passed the seeds to wedding guests and lay the fruit around marital beds to ensure a prosperous union. So although pomegranates are winter fruits, they symbolize fertility, love, and marriage, important themes for a Midsummer meal.

4 chicken breasts
1 tablespoon chili powder
½ cup pomegranate juice
¼ cup sunflower oil

Rub chili powder into chicken breasts on both sides and place in a glass dish. Mix pomegranate juice and sunflower oil. Brush both sides of chicken breasts with half the juice mixture. Grill chicken breasts over hot coals, basting with remaining marinade until cooked through.

Berry Bowl Bouquets

Nothing says summer like colorful berries and fragrant flowers. This treat combines both in a refreshing, light dessert.

1 pint each, strawberries, blueberries, raspberries
1 cup each pesticide-free violets, strawberry blossoms, and dianthus flowers
1 cup superfine sugar

Wash all fruit and flowers. Hull and slice strawberries. In a pretty bowl, gently toss together berries and flowers. Sprinkle with sugar and chill until ready to serve.

Sun Drops

Legend has it that the sunflower was once a water nymph so in love with Apollo, god of the Sun, that she gazed up at his golden chariot hour after hour, day after day, trailing his every move with the tilt of her head. She sat so long that her limbs transformed into roots and her golden hair and round face became the head of a sunflower, still following the sun.

½ cup butter, softened
½ cup white sugar

1 egg, beaten
2 tablespoons fresh lemon juice
1 tablespoon vanilla
½ cup ground sunflower seeds
1 teaspoon lemon zest
1 ¼ cups all-purpose flour

2 to 3 drops lemon food coloring (optional)

Preheat oven to 350. In a large bowl, cream together butter and sugar. Beat in egg, lemon juice, vanilla, sunflower seeds, zest, and food coloring. Gradually mix in the flour until well blended. Round into balls and place on an ungreased cookie sheet. Bake 8 to 10 minutes or until cookies are lightly colored.

Mead Punch

Mead is a sweet honey wine, often incorporated with herbs, spices, and fruit. Some cultures refer to the full June moon as the "mead" moon or "honey" moon, hence the popular term for the vacation a bride and groom embark on after they take their vows.

1 quart white grape juice
4 cups honey
1 cup sweet woodruff leaves, rinsed
2 bottles white wine, chilled
1 liter soda water, chilled
1 cup chamomile blossoms, rinsed

In a large saucepan, gently heat grape juice, honey, and woodruff until the honey dissolves. Strain woodruff and chill juice mixture for one hour. When the guests arrive, empty honeyed juice, wine, and soda water into a large punch bowl. Float chamomile flowers on top and serve.

Sun Tea

Busy schedules and modern conveniences often make us forget just how magical the sun can be. Harness the power of the great star by preparing a batch of this herbal tea.

6 to 8 cups fresh herbs, washed
Water

Fill a glass tea jug with your favorite herbs and edible flowers for tea. Use a variety. I like to combine lavender, mint, and rose petals. Other combinations can include lemon balm, stevia, sage, hyssop, fennel, scented geranium leaves, and thyme. Place the jug in a sunny spot and let the sun penetrate it all day. Sweeten tea with sugar or honey and serve over ice.

Acknowledgments

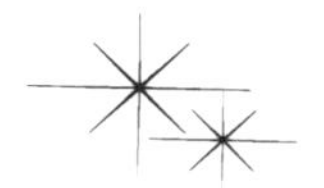

I want to thank Jeff Bezos for creating Kindle Direct Publishing and allowing this writer to find her audience when no one else would. Thanks also to Terry Goodman, who took a chance on a self-published author who will always be grateful. Your guidance made the entire transition so much easier than I thought it would be. Thanks also to my editor, Alison Dasho, for keen insight and gentle suggestions that improved this book tremendously. To the creative people who gave Stacy a make-over and put up with my change requests—you guys rock! I love my covers. And my author team, especially Jacque Ben-Zekry, thanks for taking the time to answer tedious questions expediantly and for all the conference magic you perform.

Finally, to my husband, who insists he always knew I would get here. Thank you for reading everything I write, for laughing in all the right places, the brainstorming sessions, the wine, the hand-holding, the cheers, the encouragement, the advice, and the unwavering positivity. Most of all, thanks for believing.

About the Author

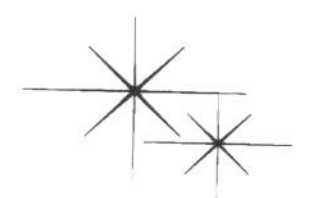

Photo by George Annino, 2011

Barbra Annino is a native of Chicago, a book junkie, and a Springsteen addict. She's worked as a bartender and humor columnist, and currently lives in picturesque Galena, Illinois, where she ran a bed-and-breakfast for five years. She now writes fiction full-time—when she's not walking her three Great Danes.